JUST ONE
LAST NIGHT

BY
HELEN BROOKS

First published in Great Britain 2012
by Mills & Boon, an imprint of Harlequin (UK) Limited.
Harlequin (UK) Limited, Eton House, 18-24 Paradise Road,
Richmond, Surrey TW9 1SR

© Helen Brooks 2012

ISBN: 978 0 263 22787 1

Harlequin (UK) policy is to use papers that are natural, renewable and recyclable products and made from wood grown in sustainable forests. The logging and manufacturing process conform to the legal environmental regulations of the country of origin.

Printed and bound in Great Britain
by CPI Antony Rowe, Chippenham, Wiltshire

She was *pregnant*. Pregnant with their baby.

As his face lit up Melanie strained away from him, her back pressing against the driver's door. 'No,' she mumbled, fear in her voice as well as in her body language. 'I don't want this—can't you see? This doesn't change anything between us.'

'Are you crazy?' Forde asked huskily. 'Of course it does.' And then, as her words hit home, his eyes widened. 'Let me get this right. You want the baby but you don't want me? Is that what you're trying to say?'

Her face white, Melanie shook her head. 'I don't mean that.'

'Then what the hell *do* you mean?' Knowing his voice had been too loud, and struggling for calmness, Forde took a rasping breath. 'I want to sit down and discuss this properly. You're carrying my child, Nell. I'll take you out for a meal tonight. Be ready about eight.'

She really didn't want to do this. Being with Forde was painful at the best of times, reminding her of all she'd lost. 'I don't think—'

She found her words cut off as his mouth took hers.

The kiss was a deliberate assault on her senses. She recognised that from the moment his mouth descended. But he'd taken her by surprise, and by the time reason was back she was trembling at the sweetness of his lovemaking.

Helen Brooks lives in Northamptonshire, and is married with three children and three beautiful grandchildren. As she is a committed Christian, busy housewife, mother and grandma, her spare time is at a premium, but her hobbies include reading, swimming and gardening, and walks with her husband and their two Irish terriers. Her long-cherished aspiration to write became a reality when she put pen to paper on reaching the age of forty and sent the result off to Mills & Boon.

Recent titles by the same author:

IN THE ITALIAN'S SIGHTS
THE BEAUTIFUL WIDOW
SNOWBOUND SEDUCTION
SWEET SURRENDER WITH THE MILLIONAIRE

Did you know these are also available as eBooks?
Visit www.millsandboon.co.uk

JUST ONE
LAST NIGHT

CHAPTER ONE

MELANIE stared at the letter in her hand. The heavy black scrawl danced before her eyes and she had to blink a few times before reading it again, unable to believe what her brain was telling her.

Didn't Forde understand that this was impossible? Absolutely ridiculous? In fact it was so nonsensical she read the letter a third time to convince herself she wasn't dreaming. She had recognised his handwriting as soon as she'd picked the post off the mat and her heart had somersaulted, but she'd imagined he was writing about something to do with their divorce. Instead...

Melanie breathed in deeply, telling herself to calm down.

Instead Forde had written to ask her to consider doing some work for him. Well, not him exactly, she conceded reluctantly. His mother. But it was part and parcel of the same thing. They hadn't spoken in months and then, cool as a cucumber, he wrote out of the blue. Only Forde Masterson could be so spectacularly outrageous. He was unbelievable. Utterly unbelievable.

She threw the letter onto the table and began to open the rest of the post, finishing her toast and coffee as she did so. Her small dining room doubled as her office, an arrangement that had its drawbacks if she wanted to invite friends round for a meal. Not that she had time for a social life anyway. Since leaving Forde a few weeks into the new year, she'd put all her energy into building up the landscape design company she had started twelve months after they'd married, just after—

A shutter shot down in her mind with the inflexibility of solid steel. That time was somewhere she didn't go, had never gone since leaving Forde. It was better that way.

The correspondence dealt with, Melanie finished the last of her first pot of coffee of the day and went upstairs to her tiny bathroom to shower and get dressed before she rang James, her very able assistant, to go through what was required that day. James was a great employee inasmuch as he was full of enthusiasm and a tirelessly hard worker, but with his big-muscled body and dark good looks he attracted women like bees to a honeypot. He often turned up in the morning looking a little the worse for wear. However, it never affected his work and Melanie had no complaints.

Clad in her working clothes of denim jeans and a vest top, Melanie looped her thick, shoulder-length ash-blonde hair into a ponytail and applied plenty of sunscreen to her pale, easily burned English skin. The country was currently enjoying a heatwave and the August day was already hot at eight in the morning.

Before going downstairs again, she flung open her bedroom window and let the rich scent of the climbing roses outside fill the room. The cottage was tiny—just her bedroom and a separate bathroom upstairs, and a pocket-size sitting room and the dining room downstairs, the latter opening into a new extension housing a kitchen overlooking the minute courtyard garden. But Melanie loved it. The courtyard's dry stone walls were hidden beneath climbing roses and honeysuckle, which covered the walls at the back of the cottage too, and the paved area that housed her small bistro table and two chairs was a blaze of colour from the flowering pots surrounding its perimeter. In the evenings it was bliss to eat her evening meal out there in the warm, soft air with just the twittering of the birds and odd bee or butterfly for company. It wasn't too extreme to say this little cottage had saved her sanity in the first crucifyingly painful days after she'd fled the palatial home she'd shared with Forde.

The cottage was one in the middle of a terrace of ten, all occupied by couples or single folk and half of them—like the ones either side of Melanie—used as weekend bolt-holes by London high-flyers who retreated to the more gentle pace of life south-west of the capital, where the villages and towns still retained an olde-worlde charm. It was also sixty miles or so distant from Forde's house in Kingston upon Thames, sufficient mileage, Melanie had felt, to avoid the prospect of running into him by chance.

She had wondered if her fledgling business would survive when she'd moved, but in actual fact it had thrived so well she had been able to take on James within a month or two of leaving the city. The nature of the work had changed a little; when she had been based in Kingston upon Thames she'd been involved with the layout of housing areas with play facilities and general urban regeneration. Now it was mostly public and private garden work, along with forest landscaping and land reclamation. Some of the time she and James worked with members of a team that could include architects, planners, civil engineers and quantity surveyors depending upon what the job involved. On other projects they worked in isolation on private gardens or country estates. Inevitably office work was part of the deal, along with site visits and checking progress of work where other bodies were involved.

Becoming aware she was in danger of daydreaming, Melanie turned away from the window, her mind jumping into gear and detailing what the day involved.

James was due to oversee the bulldozing of a number of ancient pigsties, which the client wanted transformed into a wild flower garden, being concerned about the loss of natural habitats in the countryside in general and in the surrounding area of the old farmhouse he'd bought in particular. Melanie had suggested a meadow effect, created with a profusion of wild flowers growing in turf on soil that was low in fertility, the mowing regime of which had to allow the flowers to seed before being cut.

In stark contrast, she was off to put the finishing touches to a formal garden she and James had been working on for three weeks. It was a place of calm order, expressed in a carefully balanced treatment of space and symmetry, the details of which had been all-important. The retired bank manager and his wife who had purchased the property recently in the midst of a small country town had been delighted with her initial plan of a neat lawn and matching paved areas at either end of the grass, clipped bushes and trained plants—along with fruit trees in restricted shapes—providing a gentle approach to the precise layout they'd first requested.

She loved her job. Melanie breathed a silent prayer of thankfulness. Devising a personal creation for each individual client was so satisfying, along with reconciling their ideas with the practical potential of the available plot. Not that this was always easy, especially if a client had seen their 'perfect' garden in a magazine or brochure, which inevitably was bigger or smaller than the space they had available. But then that was part of the challenge and fun.

Half smiling to herself as her mind skimmed over several such past clients, Melanie made her way downstairs, pausing at the door to the dining room. It was only then she acknowledged that since reading Forde's letter, every single word had been burning in her brain.

Dear Melanie,
I'm writing to ask a favour, not for myself but for Isabelle.

Typical Forde, she thought darkly, her heart thudding as she glanced at the letter lying on the table. No 'how are you?' or any other such social nicety. Just straight to the point.

She hasn't been too well lately and the garden at Hillview is too much for her, not that she would ever admit it. The whole thing needs complete changing with an emphasis on low maintenance now she's nearly eighty. The trouble is she won't even allow a gardener onto the premises so I've

no chance of persuading her to let strangers do
an overhaul. But she'd trust you. Think about it,
would you? And ring me.
Forde

Think about it! Melanie shook her head. She didn't
have to think about it to know what she was going to
do, and there was no way she was going to ring Forde
either. She had insisted on no contact between them
and that still held.

Walking over to the table, she picked up the piece
of paper and the envelope and ripped them into small
pieces, throwing the fragments into the bin. There.
Finished with. She had enough to do today without
thinking about Forde and his ridiculous request.

She stood for a moment more, staring into space.
What did he mean when he'd said Isabelle hadn't been
well? She pictured Forde's sweet-faced mother in her
mind as her heart lurched. It had been almost as bad
walking out of Isabelle's life as that of her son all those
months ago, but she had known all threads holding her
to Forde had to be severed if she had any chance of
making it. She'd written a brief note to her mother-in-
law, making it clear she didn't expect Isabelle to understand but that she'd had good reasons for doing what
she'd done and that it hadn't altered the genuine love
and respect she had for the older woman. She had asked
Isabelle not to reply. When she had, Melanie had returned the letter unopened. It had torn her in two to
do it, but she hadn't doubted it was the right decision.
She wouldn't put Isabelle in the position of piggy-in-
the-middle. Isabelle adored Forde, an only child, and

mother and son were closer than most, Forde's father having died when Forde was in his late teens.

Her mobile ringing brought her out of her reverie. It was James. There had been a bad accident just in front of him and he was stuck in a traffic jam that went back for miles so he was going to be late getting to the site. Was it possible she could go there and detail to the workmen exactly what needed to be done and get them started before she went on to her own job? They had the plan of work on paper but there was nothing like face-to-face instructions…

Melanie agreed. After a disaster on an early job when a perfectly sound conservatory had been demolished and the old ramshackle greenhouse had been left intact, she didn't trust workmen to take the time to read plans, and this was something she'd drummed into James from the start.

Sighing, she mentally revised her morning, decided to leave straight away rather than see to a pile of paperwork she'd hoped to sort out before she left the house, and within a few minutes was travelling towards the farmhouse in her old pickup truck. It was going to be a hectic day but that was good—if nothing else, of necessity she wouldn't have time to think about Forde's letter.

It *was* a hectic day. Melanie arrived home in deep twilight but with a big, fat cheque in her pocket from the retired couple who had been thrilled how their garden had come together. After sliding the truck into the parking space reserved for her in the square cobbled yard at one side of the row of cottages, she walked along the narrow pathway that led off the yard and along the back of the cottages, pausing at the small doorway in the long, ivy-festooned wall that led into her tiny garden. Unlocking the door, she stepped into her small haven of peace, breathing in the delicious perfume of the roses adorning the walls. She was home, and she wanted nothing more than a long, hot bath to relax her aching muscles. She had been determined to finish the job on schedule today and hadn't even stopped for a bite of lunch.

Locking the garden door, she entered the house through the kitchen as she did most days, slipping off the thick walking boots she wore on a job and leaving them on the cork mat ready for morning. Barefoot, she padded upstairs, flinging open the bathroom window so the scents of the garden could fill the room, and began to run the bath before going into the bedroom and divesting herself of her clothes.

Two minutes later she was lying in hot, soapy bubbles gazing up at a charcoal sky in which the first stars were peeping. Not for the first time she blessed the fact that the developers who had renovated the string of cottages had had soul. In placing the big, cast-iron bath under the window as they had, it meant the occupier could lie and see an ever-changing picture in the heavens through the clear glass they'd installed. Melanie never closed the blinds until she was ready to get out of the bath and on occasions like tonight, when she was tired and aching, it was bliss to lie in the dark and think of nothing. Although tonight the carefully cultivated trick of emptying her mind and totally relaxing wasn't working...

Melanie frowned, acknowledging Forde had persistently been battering at the door to her consciousness all day, however much she had tried to ignore him. And she had tried. How she'd tried. She didn't *want* any contact with him, however remote. She didn't *want* to have him invading her mind and unsettling her. He, and Isabelle too, for that matter, were the past, there was no place for them in the present and less still in the future. This was a matter of self-survival.

She heard the telephone ring downstairs but let the answer machine take a message. Forcing her tight muscles to relax, limb by limb, she slid further into the silky water, shutting her eyes. After a few minutes her mobile began playing its little tune from the pocket of her working jeans in the bedroom. It was probably James, reporting how his day had gone, but she made no attempt to find out. This was *her* time, she told herself militantly. The rest of the world could take a hike for a while.

It was another half an hour before she climbed out of the bath, and the house phone had taken another two messages by then. After washing her hair and swathing it on top of her head with a small fluffy towel, she slipped on her bathrobe. Her stomach was reminding her she hadn't eaten since the two slices of toast at breakfast, and, deciding food was a priority, she didn't bother to get dressed, making her way downstairs just as she was.

She had reached the bottom step and her tiny square of hall when a sharp knock at the front door caused Melanie to nearly jump out of her skin.

What now? She shut her eyes for an infinitesimal moment. It could only be James reporting some disaster or other after he'd been unable to reach her by phone. And that was fine, she was his boss after all, but she really had wanted to simply crash tonight. It was clearly too much to ask.

Wiping her face clear of all irritation and stitching a smile in place, she tightened the belt of her bathrobe and then opened the door.

The six-foot-four, ruggedly handsome male standing on her doorstep wasn't James.

A bolt of shock shot through her and then she froze.

'Hi.' Forde didn't smile. 'Am I interrupting something?'

'What?' She gazed at him stupidly. He looked wonderful. White shirt, black jeans, a muscled tower of brooding masculinity.

The silver-blue eyes with their thick, short, black lashes flicked to her bathrobe and then back to her stunned face. 'Are you...entertaining?'

As the full import behind his words hit, hot colour surged beneath her high cheekbones along with a reviving dose of adrenaline into her body. Her expression becoming icy, she said slowly, 'What did you say?'

Forde relaxed slightly. OK, so he'd got that wrong, then. But he had been waiting all day for a response to his letter, which had never come, and after ringing several times tonight he'd decided to see if she was ignoring him or wasn't home. There had been lights on—*upstairs*—and then she'd come to the door flustered and dressed like that, or rather *un*dressed like that. What was he supposed to think? 'I wondered if you had visitors,' he said carefully, getting ready to use his shoulder on the door if she tried to slam it in his face. 'You weren't answering the phone.'

'I was late home from work and then I had a bath—' She stopped abruptly. 'What am I explaining to you for?' she added furiously. 'And how dare you suggest I had a man here?'

'It was the obvious answer,' said Forde.

'To you, maybe, but you shouldn't judge everyone by your own standards.' She glared at him angrily.

'I'm suitably crushed.'

His mocking air was the last straw. Forde had always been the only person in the whole world who could make her so mad the cool façade she hid behind normally melted in the heat. Having been brought up in a succession of foster homes, she had learnt early on to keep her feelings hidden, but that had never worked with Forde. 'Will you please leave?' she said tightly, trying to close the door and finding his shoulder was in the way.

'Did you get my letter?' In contrast to her fury he appeared calm and composed, even relaxed. That rankled as much as his outrageous assumption she'd had a man in her bed.

Melanie nodded, giving up the struggle to close the door.

'And?' he pressed with silky smoothness.

'And what?'

He studied her with the silvery gaze that seemed to have the power to look straight into her soul. 'Don't pretend you don't care.'

For a moment she thought he was referring to him and then realised he was talking about her concern for his mother. She blinked, the anger draining away. Quietly, she said, 'How is Isabelle?'

He shrugged. 'As stubborn as a mule, as always.'

Melanie could almost have smiled. Forde's mother was a softer, more feminine version of her strong-willed, inflexible son but every bit as determined. But Isabelle had always been wonderfully supportive and loving to her, the mother she'd always longed for but never had. The thought was weakening, intensifying the ever-present ache in her heart. To combat it her voice was flat and without emotion when she said, 'You said she'd been unwell?'

'She fell and broke her hip in that damn garden of hers and then there were complications with her heart during surgery.'

Melanie's dark brown eyes opened wide. When he'd said in his letter Isabelle had been unwell she'd imagined Forde's mother had had the flu, something like that. But an operation… Isabelle could have died and she wouldn't have known. Her heart thudding, she murmured, 'I— I'm sorry.'

'Not as sorry as I am,' Forde said grimly. 'She won't do as she's told and seems hell-bent on putting herself back in hospital, refusing to come and stay with me or take it easy in a convalescent home somewhere. She was determined to return home as soon as she was discharged and against medical advice, I might add. The only concession she'd make was to let me hire a live-in nurse until she's mobile again, and that was under protest. She's impossible.'

Melanie stared at him. Forde would be exactly the same in those circumstances. He was impossible at the best of times. And easily the sexiest man on the planet.

The last thought caused her to pull the belt of her robe tighter. *Don't let him see how him being here is affecting you,* she told herself silently. *You know it's over. Be strong.* 'I'm sorry,' she said again, 'but you must see me doing any work for your mother is ridiculous, Forde. We're in the middle of a divorce.'

'*We* are. That shouldn't affect your relationship with Isabelle, surely? She was very hurt when you returned her letter unread, by the way,' he added softly.

Unfair. Below the belt. But that was Forde all over. 'It was for the best.'

'Really?' He considered her thoughtfully. 'For whom?'

'Forde, I'm not about to stand here bandying words with you.' She shivered involuntarily although the night air was warm and humid.

'You're cold.' He pushed the door fully open, causing her to instinctively step back into the hall. 'Let's discuss this inside.'

'*Excuse me?*' She recovered her wits enough to bar his way. 'I don't remember inviting you in.'

'Melanie, we've been married for two years and unless you've put on a pretty good act in all that time, you are fond of my mother. I'm asking for your help for her sake, OK? Are you really going to refuse?'

Two years, four months and five days, to be precise. And the first eleven months had been heaven on earth. After that… 'Please go,' she said weakly, much more weakly than she would have liked. 'Our solicitors wouldn't like this.'

'Damn the solicitors.' He took her arm, moving her aside as he stepped into the hall and shut the door behind him. 'Parasites, the lot of them. I need to talk to you, that's the important thing.'

He was close, so close the familiar delicious smell and feel of him were all around her, invoking memories that were seductively intimate. They brought a sheen of heat to her skin, her heartbeat speeding up and beginning to rocket in her chest. Forde was the only man she'd ever loved, and even now his power over her was mesmerising. 'Please leave,' she said firmly.

'Look,' he murmured softly, 'make some coffee and listen to me, Nell, OK? That's all I'm asking. For Isabelle's sake.'

He wasn't touching her now but her whole being was twisting in pain. Nevertheless, the harsh discipline she'd learnt as a child held good, enabling her to control the flood of emotion his old nickname for her had induced and say, a little shakily admittedly, 'This isn't a good idea, Forde.'

'On the contrary, it's an excellent idea.'

She looked at him, big and dark in her little hall, his black hair falling over his brow, and knew he wasn't going to take no for an answer. And considering he was six-feet-four of lean, honed muscle and she was a slender five-seven, she could scarcely manhandle him out of the house. She turned, saying over her shoulder, 'It doesn't seem I've much option, does it?' as she led the way into her pocket-size sitting room.

Forde followed her, secretly amazed he'd been allowed admittance without more of a fight. But, hey, he thought. Go with the flow. The first battle was over but the war was far from won.

His gaze moved swiftly over the small room, which had Melanie's stamp all over it, from the two plumpy cream sofas and matching drapes and the thick, coffee-coloured carpet, to the old but charmingly restored Victorian fireplace, which had a pile of logs stacked against it. Very stylish but definitely cosy. Modern but not glaringly so. And giving nothing of herself away. A beautiful mirror stretched across the far wall making the room appear larger, but not one picture or photograph to be seen. Nothing personal.

'Sit down and I'll get the coffee.' She waved to one of the sofas before leaving, shaking her hair free of the towel as she went.

Forde didn't take the invitation. Instead he followed her into the hall and through to the kitchen-diner. This was more lived in, the table scattered with files and papers and the draining board in the tiny kitchen holding a few plates and dishes. He dared bet she spent most of the time at home working.

Melanie had turned as he'd entered and now she followed his glance, saying quickly, 'I didn't have time to wash up this morning before I left and I was too tired last night.'

Forde pulled up one of the dining chairs, sitting astride it with his arms draped over the back as he said easily, 'You don't have to apologise to me.'

'I wasn't. I was explaining.'

It was curt and he mentally acknowledged the tone. Ignoring the hostility, he smiled. 'Nice little place you've got here.'

Her eyes met his and he could see she was deciding whether he was being genuine or not. He saw her shoulders relax slightly and knew she'd taken his observation the way it had been meant.

'Thank you,' she said quietly. 'I like it.'

'Janet sends her regards, by the way.'

Janet was Forde's very able cook and cleaner who came in for a few hours each day to wash and iron, keep the house clean and prepare the evening meal. She was a merry little soul, in spite of having a husband who had never done a day's honest work in his life and three teenage children who ate her out of house and home. Melanie had liked her very much. Janet had been with her on the day of the accident and had sat and held her until the ambulance had arrived—

She brought her thoughts to a snapping halt. *Don't think of that. Not now.* Woodenly, she said, 'Tell her hello from me.' Drawing in a deep breath and feeling she needed something stronger than coffee to get through the next little while, she opened the fridge. 'There's some wine chilled if you'd prefer a glass to coffee?'

'Great. Thanks.' He rose as he spoke, walking and opening the back door leading onto the shadowed courtyard. 'This is nice. Shall we drink out here?'

She was trying very, very hard to ignore the fact she was stark naked under the robe but it was hard with her body responding to him the way it always did. He'd always only had to look at her for her blood to sing in her veins and her whole being melt. Forde was one of those men who had a natural magnetism that oozed masculinity; it was in his walk, his smile, every move he made. The height and breadth of him were impressive, and she knew full well there wasn't an ounce of fat on the lean, muscled body, but it was his face—too rugged to be pretty-boy handsome but breathtakingly attractive, nonetheless—that drew any woman from sixteen to ninety. Hard and strong, with sharply defined planes and angles unsoftened by his jet-black hair and piercing silvery eyes, his face was sexy and cynical, and his slightly crooked mouth added to his charm.

Dynamite. That was what one of her friends had called him when they'd first begun dating, and she'd been right. But dynamite was powerful and dangerous, she told herself ruefully, taking the opportunity to run her hands through the thick silk of her hair and bring it into some kind of order.

When she stepped into the scented shadows with two glasses and the bottle of wine, Forde was already sitting at the bistro table, his long legs spread out in front of him and his head tilted back as he looked up at the riot of climbing roses covering the back of the house. They, together with the fragrant border plants in the pots, perfumed the still warm air with a sweet heaviness. Another month or so and the weather would begin to cool and the first chill of autumn make itself felt.

It had been snowing that day when she'd left Forde. Seven months had passed. Seven months without Forde in her life, in her bed…

She sat down carefully after placing the glasses on the table, pulling the folds of the robe round her legs and wishing she'd taken the time to nip upstairs and get dressed. But that would have looked as though she expected him to stay and she wanted him to leave as soon as possible.

The thought mocked her and she had to force her eyes not to feast on him. She had been aching to see him again; he'd filled her dreams every night since the split and sometimes she had spent hours sitting out here in the darkness while the rest of the world was asleep after a particularly erotic fantasy that had left her unable to sleep again.

'How are you?' His rich, smoky voice brought her eyes to his dark face.

She reached for her glass and took a long swallow before she said, 'Fine. And you?'

'Great, just great.' His voice dripped sarcasm. 'My wife walks out on me citing irreconcilable differences and then threatens to get a restraining order when I attempt to make her see reason over the next weeks—'

'You were phoning umpteen times a day and turning up everywhere,' she interrupted stiffly. 'It was obsessional.'

'What did you expect? I know things changed after the accident but—'

'Don't.' This time she cut him short by jumping to her feet, her eyes wild. 'I don't want to discuss this, Forde. If that's why you've come, you can leave now.'

'Damn it, Nell.' He raked his hand through his hair, taking a visibly deep breath as he struggled to control his emotions. A few screamingly tense moments ticked by and then his voice came, cool and calm. 'Sit down and drink your wine. I came here to discuss you taking on the garden at Hillview and making it easy for my mother to manage it. That's all.'

'I think it's better you go.'

'Tough.' He eyed her sardonically, his mouth twisting.

Her nostrils flared. 'You really are the most arrogant man on the planet.' And unfortunately the most attractive.

Forde shrugged. 'I can live with that—it's a small planet.' He took a swallow of wine. 'Sit down,' he said again, 'and stop behaving like a Victorian heroine in a bad movie. Let me explain how things stand with

Mother at present before you decide one way or the other, OK?'

She sat, not because she wanted to but because there was really nothing else she could do.

'Along with her damaged hip she's got a heart problem, Nell, but the main problem is Isabelle herself. I actually caught her trying to prune back some bush or other a couple of days ago. She'd sneaked out of the house when the nurse was busy. I've offered to get her a gardener or do the work myself but she won't have it, although under pressure she admits It's getting overgrown and that upsets her. When I suggested it needs landscaping she reluctantly agreed and then flatly refused to have what she called clod-hopping strangers tramping everywhere. You can bet your boots once the nurse is no longer needed in a couple of weeks she'll be out there doing goodness knows what. I shall arrive one day and find her collapsed or worse. There's nearly an acre of ground all told, as you know—it's too much for her.'

He was really worried; she could see that. Melanie stared at him, biting her lip. And she knew how passionate Isabelle was about her garden; when she had still been with Forde she and his mother had spent hours working together in the beautiful grounds surrounding the old house. But what had been relatively easy for Isabelle to manage thirty, twenty, even ten years ago, was a different story now. But Isabelle would pine and lose hope if she couldn't get out in her garden. What needed to be done was a totally new plan for the grounds with an emphasis on low maintenance, but even then, if they were to keep the mature trees Isabelle loved so dearly, Forde's mother would have to agree to a gardener coming in at certain times of the year to deal with the falling leaves and other debris. And she really couldn't see Isabelle agreeing to that, unless…

Thinking out loud, she said slowly, 'I'd obviously need to make a proper assessment of the site, but looking to the future, James, the young man who works for me, is very personable. All the old ladies love him.' The young ones as well. 'If Isabelle got to know him, perhaps she'd agree to him coming in for a day or two once a month to maintain the new garden, which I'd design with a view to minimum upkeep.'

Forde shifted in his seat. 'You'll do it, then?' he said softly. 'You'll take on the job?'

Melanie brought her eyes to his face. There was something in his gaze that reminded her—as if she didn't know—that she was playing with fire. Quickly, a veil slid over her own expression. 'On certain conditions.'

One black eyebrow quirked. 'I might have guessed. Nothing is straightforward with you. OK, so what are these conditions? Nothing too onerous, I trust?'

It was too intimate—the hushed surroundings enclosing them in their own tiny world, the perfumed air washing over her senses, Forde's big male body just inches away, and—not least—her nakedness under the robe. This sort of situation was exactly what she'd strived to avoid by not seeing him over the last torturous months. She really shouldn't have let him in.

She gulped down the last of her wine and poured another for Dutch courage. Forde's glass was half-full but he put his hand over the rim when she went to top it up. 'Driving,' he said shortly, settling back in his seat and crossing one leg over the other knee. 'Spell out your demands,' he added, when she still didn't speak. 'Don't be shy.'

The sarcasm helped, stiffening her backbone and her resolve, but she still felt as though she was standing on the edge of a precipice. One false move and she'd be lost.

'But before you do...' He moved swiftly, taking her hand before she had time to pull away and holding it fast in his own strong fingers as he leaned across the table. 'Do you still love me, Nell?'

CHAPTER TWO

IT WAS so typical Forde Masterson! She should have
been expecting it, should have been aware he'd take
her off guard sooner or later. His ruthless streak had
taken the fledgling property-developing business he'd
started in his bedroom at the family home when he
was eighteen years old, using an inheritance left to him
by his grandmother, into a multimillion-pound enter-
prise in just sixteen years. His friends called him inex-
orable, single-minded, immovable; his enemies had a
whole host of other names, but even they had to admit
they'd rather deal with Forde than some of the sharks
in the property-developing game. He could be merci-
less when the occasion warranted it but his word was
his bond, and that was increasingly rare in the cut and
thrust of business.

Melanie stared into the dark, handsome face just
inches from hers. His eyes shone mother-of-pearl in
the dim light, their expression inscrutable. Somehow she
managed to say, 'I told you I'm not discussing us, Forde.'

'I didn't ask for a discussion. A simple yes or no
would suffice.' Black eyebrows rose mockingly.

She moved her head, allowing the pale curtain of
her hair to swing forward, hiding her face as she jerked

her hand free. 'This is pointless. It's over—*we're* over. Accept it and move on. I have.' *Liar.*

'You still haven't answered my question.'

'I don't have to.' In an effort to control the trembling deep inside she reached out her hand and picked up her glass of wine, taking several long sips and praying her hand wouldn't shake. 'This is *my* house, remember? I make the rules.'

'The trouble is, you never did believe in happy endings, did you, Nell?' Forde said softly.

Her head jerked up as his words hit home and then he watched a shutter click down over her expression. She had always been able to do that, mask what she was thinking and adopt a distant air, but nine times out of ten he'd broken through the defence mechanism she used to keep people at bay. He knew her childhood had been tough; orphaned at the age of three, she couldn't remember her parents. Her maternal grandmother had taken her in initially but when she, too, had tragically died a year later, none of Melanie's other relations had stepped up to the mark. One foster home after another had ensued and Melanie admitted herself she'd been a troubled little girl and quite a handful. When he had fallen in love with her he had wanted to make that all better. He still wanted to. The only obstacle was Melanie herself, and it was one hell of an obstacle.

'From the first day we met you were waiting for us to fall apart,' he continued in the same quiet tone. 'Waiting for it to all go wrong. I didn't realise that until recently. I don't know why. There were enough indicators early on.'

She spoke through clenched teeth. 'I don't know what you are talking about.'

He studied her thoughtfully as she finished her second glass of wine. Her voice and body language belied her blank face. Underneath that formidable barrier she presented, that of a capable, strong businesswoman and woman of the world, Melanie was scared. Of him. He had acknowledged it at the same time he'd come to the conclusion she had never believed they'd make old bones together. She had loved and trusted him, he knew that, but he also knew now that those feelings had made her feel vulnerable and frightened. She had been on her own emotionally all her life before they'd met—twenty-five years—and that tough shell had been hard to break, but he'd done it. She had let him in. But not far enough, or they wouldn't be in this mess right now.

Following through on his thoughts, he said, 'I blamed myself at first after the accident, you know—for the distance between us, for the way every conversation fragmented or turned into a row. Stupid, but I didn't understand you'd made the decision to shut me out and nothing short of a nuclear explosion could have changed things.'

She didn't say a word. In fact she could have been carved in stone. A beautiful stone statue without feelings or emotion.

'The accident—'

'Stop talking about the *accident*,' she said woodenly. Although she had been the one to insist they called it that. 'It was a miscarriage. I was stupid enough to fall downstairs and I killed our son.'

'Nell—'

'No.' She held up her hand, palm facing him. 'Let's face facts here. That is what happened, Forde. He was born too early and they couldn't save him. Another few weeks and it might have been all right, but at twenty-two weeks he didn't stand a chance. I was supposed to nurture him and keep him safe and I failed him.'

In one way he was glad she was talking about it; she'd refused to in the past, locking her emotions away from him and everyone else. In another sense he was appalled at the way even now, over sixteen months later, she was totally blaming herself. She had been a little light-headed that morning and had stayed in bed late after he'd left for work, Janet having brought her up a breakfast tray some time around ten o'clock. At half-past ten Janet had heard a terrible scream and a crash and rushed from the kitchen into the hall, to find Melanie lying twisted and partially conscious at the foot of the stairs, the contents of the tray scattered about her.

It had been an accident. Tragic, devastating, but an accident nonetheless, but from the time their son had been stillborn some hours later Melanie had retreated into herself. He hadn't been able to comfort her, in fact she'd barely let him near her and at times he was sure she'd hated him, probably because he was a reminder of all they'd lost. And so they'd struggled on month after miserable month, Melanie burying herself in the business she'd started and working all hours until he was lucky if he saw her for more than an hour each night, and he— Forde's mouth set grimly. He'd been in hell. He was still in hell, come to it.

He wanted to say, 'Accidents happen,' but that was too trite in the circumstances. Instead he stood up, drawing her stiff, unyielding body into his arms. 'You would have given your life for his if you could have,' he said softly. 'No one holds you responsible for what happened, Nell, don't you see?'

Melanie drew in a shuddering breath. 'Please go now.'

She felt brittle in his grasp; she was too thin, much too thin, and even as he held her she swayed slightly as though she was going to pass out. 'What's the matter?' He stared into her white face. 'Are you unwell?'

She looked at him, her eyes focusing, and he realised she was holding onto him for support. 'I—I think I must be a little tipsy,' she murmured dazedly. 'I missed lunch and I haven't eaten yet, and two glasses of wine…'

Hence the reason she'd spoken about the miscarriage, but, hell, if he needed to keep her in a permanent state of intoxication to break through that iron shield, he would. He gentled his voice when he said, 'Come indoors, I'll get you something.'

'No, I can manage. I— I'll ring you.'

There was no way on earth he was walking out of here right now, not when they were talking—properly talking—for the first time since Matthew's death. For a second a bolt of pain shot through him as he remembered his son, so tiny and so perfect, and then he controlled himself. He said nothing as he led her into the house and when he pushed her down on one of the dining room chairs and walked into the kitchen, she made no protest. He rifled the fridge before turning to face her. 'OK, I can make a fairly passable cheese omelette—' He stopped abruptly. Tears were washing down her face.

With a muttered oath he reached her side, lifting her against him and holding her close as he murmured all the things he'd been wanting to say for months. That he loved her, that she was everything to him, that life was nothing without her and that the accident hadn't been her fault…

Melanie clung to him, all defences down, drinking in the strength, the hard maleness, the familiar smell of him and needing him as she'd never needed him before. She had never loved anyone else and she knew she never would; Forde was all she had ever wanted and more. At the back of her mind she knew there was a reason she should draw away but it was melting in the wonder of being in his arms, of feeling and touching him after all the months apart.

'Kiss me.' Her voice was a whisper as she raised her head and looked into his hard, handsome face. 'Show me you love me.'

He lowered his mouth to hers, brushing her lips in a tender, feather-light kiss, but as she blatantly asked for more by kissing him back passionately, her mouth opening to him, the tempo changed.

She heard him groan, felt all restraint go and then he was kissing her like a drowning man, ravaging her mouth in an agony of need. When he whisked her off her feet, holding her close to his chest, his mouth not leaving hers, she lay supine, no thought of escape in her head.

Their lovemaking had always been the stuff dreams were made of and she'd been without him for so long, she thought dizzily. She needed to taste him again, experience his hands and mouth on her body, feel him inside her…

She was barely aware of Forde carrying her up the stairs but then she was lying on the scented linen of her bed and he was beside her, the darkness broken only by the faint light from the window. He continued to kiss her as he tore off his clothes in frantic haste, caressing the side of her neck, the hollow under her ear with his burning lips before taking her mouth again in a searing kiss that made her moan with need of him.

Her robe had come undone and now he slipped it off her completely, his voice almost a growl as he murmured, 'My beautiful one, my incomparable love...'

There was no coherent thought in her head, just a longing to be closer still, and the fierceness of his desire matched hers. They touched and tasted with a sweet violence that had them both writhing and twisting as though they would consume each other, and when he plunged inside her she called out his name as her body convulsed in tune with his. Their release was as fierce and tumultuous as their lovemaking, wave after wave of unbearable pleasure sending them over the edge into a world of pure sensation, where there was no past and no future, just the blinding light and heat of the present.

Forde continued to hold her as the frantic pounding of their hearts quietened, murmuring intimate words of love as their breathing steadied. Her eyes closed, she settled herself more comfortably in the circle of his arms as she'd done so many times in the past after a night of loving, her thick brown lashes feathering the delicate skin under her eyes as she sighed softly. Within moments she was fast asleep, a sleep of utter exhaustion.

Forde's eyes had accustomed to the deep shadows and now he lifted himself on one elbow, his gaze drinking in each feature of her face. Her skin was pure milk and roses, her eyelids fragile ovals of ivory under fine, curving brows and her lips full and sensuous. He carefully stroked a strand of silky blonde hair from her brow, unable to believe that what had happened in the last hour was real.

He had had women before he'd met Melanie, and when he'd first seen her at a mutual friend's wedding he'd thought all he wanted to do was possess her like the others, enjoy a no-strings affair for as long as it lasted. By the end of their first date he'd fallen deeply in love and found himself in a place he'd never been before. They had married three months later on her twenty-sixth birthday and taken a long honeymoon in the Caribbean, which had been a magical step out of time.

His body hardened as he remembered the nights spent wrapped in each other's arms. For the first time he'd understood the difference between sex and making love, and he'd known he never wanted to be without this woman again for a moment of time.

They had returned to England where Melanie had spent the next little while giving his house in Kingston upon Thames a complete makeover to turn it into their home, rather than the very masculine bachelor residence he'd inhabited. She had given up her job working for a garden contractor when they'd got married; Melanie had wanted to try for a baby straight away and whatever she'd wanted was fine with him. He knew her history, the fact she'd never had a family home or people to call her own, and had understood how much she wanted her own children, little people who were a product of their love.

He frowned in the darkness, still studying her sleeping face. What he *hadn't* understood, not then, was that her haste to start a family was motivated more by fear than anything else. She'd been like a deprived child in a sweet shop cramming its mouth with everything in sight because it was terrified it would soon find itself locked outside once again in the cold.

And then the miscarriage happened.

He groaned in his soul, shutting his eyes for a moment against the blackness of that time.

And everything had changed. Melanie had changed. He felt he'd lost his wife as well as his child that day. He hadn't doubted at first that he would get through to her, loving her as he did, but as weeks and then months had gone by and the wall she'd erected between them had been impenetrable he'd begun to wonder. When he had returned home one night and found her gone—clothes, shoes, toiletries, every personal possession she had—and read the note she'd left stating she wanted a divorce, it almost hadn't come as a surprise.

He had been so angry that night. Angry that she could leave him when he knew nothing on earth could have made him leave her. And bereft, desperate, frantic with fear for her.

Melanie stirred slightly before curling even closer, her head on his chest and her hair fanning her face. His arms tightened round her; she seemed so small, so fragile, so young, but in part that was deceptive. She had walked away from him and made a new life for herself over the last months, managing perfectly well without him. Whereas he… He had been merely existing.

He hadn't expected this tonight. Hell, the understatement of the year, he thought wryly. Would she regret it in the morning? His chin nuzzled the silk of her hair.

He'd have to make damn sure she didn't, he told himself grimly. He had told her, in one of their furious rows after she had first left him when she had been staying with friends, that he would never let her go, and he meant it. But he'd also seen then that she was at the end of her tether, mentally, physically and emotionally. So he'd drawn back, given her space. But enough was enough. Tonight had proved she still wanted him physically however she felt about their marriage, and that was a start.

He lay perfectly still in the darkness while Melanie slept, the acutely intelligent and astute mind that had taken him from relative obscurity to fabulous wealth in just a few short years dissecting every word, every gesture, every embrace, every kiss they'd shared. When the sky began to lighten outside the window he was still awake, only finally drifting off after the birds had finished the dawn chorus, Melanie still held close to his heart.

CHAPTER THREE

THE sun was well and truly up when Melanie's eyes eased open after the first solid night's sleep she'd had since leaving Forde. She had slept so deeply that for a moment she was only semiconscious, and then memories of the previous night slammed into her mind at the same time as she became aware that she was curled into the source of her contentment.

Forde.

Frozen with horror, she stiffened, petrified Forde would open his eyes, but the steady measured vibration beneath her cheek didn't pause, and after a moment she cautiously raised her head. He was fast asleep.

She disentangled herself slowly, pausing to look into his face. Her gaze took in the familiar planes and hollows, made much more boyish in slumber; the straight nose, high cheekbones, crooked mouth with its hint of sensuality even in repose, and the dark stubble on his chin. A very determined chin. Like the man himself.

How could she have been so unbelievably stupid as to sleep with him again? Her breath caught in her throat as her stomach twisted. And it was no good blaming the wine. She had wanted him last night; she had ached and yearned for him since the time they'd parted, more to the point.

But she didn't *need* him, she told herself stonily. She had proved that; she had lived without him for seven months, hadn't she? And she was getting by.

She had barely survived losing Matthew. She had wanted nothing more than to die, the grief and guilt crucifying. She didn't ever want to be in a place where something like that could happen again. She *wouldn't* be in such a place.

She slid carefully out of bed, the trembling that had started in the pit of her stomach spreading to her limbs. She had to get out of the house before Forde woke up. It was cowardly and mean and selfish, but she *had* to. She loved him too much to let him hope they could make a go of their marriage. It was over, dead, burnt into ashes with no chance of being resurrected. It had died the moment she'd begun to fall down those stairs.

But he *would* be hoping, a little voice in the back of her mind reminded her relentlessly as she gathered her clothes together as silently as a mouse. Of course he would. As mixed messages went, this one was the pièce de résistance.

Once in the kitchen she dressed swiftly, scared any moment there would be movement from upstairs. Then she wrote him a note, hating herself for the cruelty but knowing if she faced him this morning she would dissolve in floods of tears and the whole sorry mess would just escalate.

Forde, I don't know how to put this except that I'm more sorry than I can say for behaving the way

I did last night. It was all me, I know that, and it was inexcusable.

Melanie paused, her stomach in a giant knot as she considered her next words. But there was no kind way to say it.

I can't do the together thing any more and that's nothing to do with you as a person. Again, it's all me, but it's only fair to tell you my mind is made up about the divorce. I'll still do the work for Isabelle if you want me to. Ring me about it tonight. But no more visits. That's the first condition.

Again she hesitated. How did you finish a note like this? Especially after what they'd shared the night before.

Tears were burning at the backs of her eyes but she blinked them away determinedly. Then she wrote simply:

I hope at some time in the future you can forgive me.
Nell

She owed him the intimacy of the nickname at least, she thought wretchedly, feeling lower than anything that might crawl out from under a stone. He had been attempting to comfort her last night when they'd first come into the house, and she had practically begged him to make love to her. She had instigated it all; she knew that.

Creeping upstairs, she placed the note on top of the clothes he'd discarded so frantically the night before but without looking at him again. She couldn't bear to.

It was only when she was driving away from the house that the avalanche of tears she'd been holding at bay burst forth. She managed to find a lay-by that was hidden from the road by a row of trees once she'd entered it, and cut the engine.

Steeped in misery made all the worse by the remorse and self-condemnation she was feeling, she cried until there were no more tears left. Then she wiped her eyes and blew her nose and got out of the car to compose herself in the warm, fresh air. The chirping of the birds in their busy morning activities in the trees bordering the lay-by registered after a minute or two, and she raised her eyes, searching out a flock of sparrows who were making all the noise.

Life was so simple for them, for all the animal kingdom. It was only Homo sapiens, allegedly the superior species, who made things complex.

The fragrance of Forde still lingered on her skin, the taste of him on her lips. Hugging her arms about her, she recalled how it had felt to have him inside her again, taking her to heaven and back. Falling asleep with her head on his chest, close to the steady beat of his heart, had felt like coming home and had been as pleasurable as their lovemaking.

She straightened, her soft mouth setting. She wasn't going to think about this. She was too early to arrive at the farmhouse where she and James would be working for the next week or so, but there was a café on the way that would be open. She'd go and buy herself breakfast.

The café only had one other occupant when she pushed open the door, a lorry driver who was reading his paper while he shovelled food into his mouth. After ordering a round of bacon sandwiches and a pot of tea, Melanie made her way to the ladies' cloakroom, locking the door behind her. The small room held a somewhat ancient washbasin besides the lavatory, and she peered into the speckled mirror above it. She'd looped her hair into a ponytail before leaving the house but it was in dire need of attention. And she hadn't showered or brushed her teeth.

Stripping off her clothes, she had a wash with the hard green soap, which was as ancient as the washbasin, before drying herself with several of the paper towels in the rusty dispenser. Dressing quickly, she brushed her hair and redid her ponytail before applying plenty of the sunscreen she always carried in her handbag. Brushing her teeth would have to wait.

She was about to leave the cloakroom when she glanced at herself in the mirror again and then drew closer, arrested by the look in her eyes. She blinked, unnerved by the haunting sadness. Was that what Forde had seen? Worse, was that why he had stayed and made love to her? He'd stated quite clearly that the only reason he had come to see her was to discuss the work he wanted her to undertake for Isabelle. Had he felt sorry for her? He had left her severely alone since the time she'd threatened to take out a restraining order; maybe he was seeing other women now?

Feeling emotionally sick, she left the cloakroom and

went into the main part of the café. The lorry driver had left but a group of motorbike enthusiasts were clustered around three tables, talking and laughing. She saw them glance her way but, after one swift glance, kept her head down. Dressed in leathers and with tattoos covering most of their visible flesh, they were a little intimidating, as were the huge machines parked outside next to her beaten-up old truck.

The waitress brought her sandwich and tea immediately as she sat down. Aware her eyes were still puffy from the storm of weeping, Melanie forced down the food as quickly as she could and drank one cup of tea before standing up to leave. She had just reached the door when someone tapped her on the shoulder and she turned sharply to find a huge, bearded biker behind her.

'Your bag, love,' he said, holding out her handbag, which she realised she'd left on a chair, the keys to the car being in her pocket. And then, his eyes narrowing, he added, 'You all right?'

'Yes, yes, th-thank you,' she stammered, feeling ridiculous.

'You sure?'

His blue eyes were kind under great winged eyebrows, and, pulling herself together, Melanie managed a smile. 'I'm fine, and thank you for noticing the bag,' she said, silently acknowledging this was an apt lesson in not going by appearances.

He grinned. 'I'm well trained, love. My girlfriend's the same. Forget her head, she would, if it wasn't screwed on.'

Once on the road again, Melanie gave herself a stern talking-to. The biker had asked if she was all right and the honest answer would have been no, she doubted if she would ever be what he termed 'all right' again, but that was nobody's fault but her own. She should have known better than to marry Forde and try to be like everyone else. She *wasn't* like everyone else.

She passed a young mother pushing a baby in a pushchair and bit hard on her lip. It still hurt her, seeing mothers with babies. Like a knife driven straight through her heart.

Throughout her life, every person she had loved had been taken from her in the worst possible way. First her parents, then her grandmother, even her best friend at school—her only friend, come to it, because she hadn't been a particularly sociable child—had drowned while on holiday abroad with her parents. She could still remember the numbing shock she had felt when the headmaster had announced Pam's death in assembly, and the feeling that somehow the tragedy was connected with Pam's friendship with her.

If she hadn't married Forde and wanted his baby, Matthew wouldn't have died. She had tempted fate, thought she could escape the inevitable and because of that Forde's heart had been broken as well as hers. She would never forget the look on his face when he'd held that tiny body in the palms of his hands. That was the moment she had known she had to let him go, make him free to find happiness somewhere else. Forde had said last night that she would have given her life for Matthew's if she could and he was right, but she hadn't been able to. But she could protect Forde from more hurt by exiting his life. Once the divorce was through she would move again, far away, perhaps even abroad, and in time he would meet someone else he could commit to. Women fell over themselves to get his attention and he was a passionate and very physical man. Whatever the cost in the present, this was the right thing to do for the future. *And there could be no more incidents like last night.*

Her mind irrevocably made up, Melanie felt slightly better. She had to be cruel to be kind. It was the only way.

Forde awoke suddenly with the presentiment that something was wrong. For a moment he couldn't reconcile where he was and then he remembered, turning to see that the place next to him in the bed was empty. The house was quiet and still, no sound from the bathroom or downstairs, and he let out a breath he didn't know he'd been holding.

Glancing at his watch, he saw it was gone nine o'clock and he swore softly, cursing the fact he hadn't woken before her as he swung his feet out of bed, running a hand through his sleep-tousled hair. Damn it, this was exactly what he'd wanted to prevent. But maybe she was having breakfast in the tiny courtyard garden they'd sat in the night before?

As naked as the day he was born, he took the stairs two at a time, but even before he opened the back door and looked into Melanie's tiny garden snoozing in the sun he knew she wasn't around. The small house was devoid of her presence, as if the heart of it was missing.

Cursing some more, he retraced his steps, and this time, as soon as he entered her bedroom, he saw the note on top of his clothes, which she had folded neatly for him. It was a single piece of cream-coloured paper and, sitting down on the side of the bed, he began to read it.

His stomach muscles contracted, as though a cold, hard fist was squeezing his gut. So nothing had changed. After all they'd shared last night, the fire, the passion, she was still intent on divorcing him.

Screwing the paper into a ball, he flung it across the room before getting to his feet and reaching for his clothes. He needed to get out of her house fast before he gave in to the crazy urge to break something.

Once downstairs again he relocked the back door and left by the front one, which had a Yale lock, slamming it hard behind him. His Aston Martin was waiting for him in the small car park and after sliding into the car he sat, the door wide open and his hands on the steering wheel.

Where did he go from here? This morning had been a repeat of so many mornings when he'd awakened from erotic dreams of their lovemaking and reached out for her across an empty expanse of bed, only for reality to slam in. But this morning had been different. Last night had been real. She'd been silk and honey in his arms, her body opening to him and accommodating him perfectly as he'd thrust them both to a climax of unbearable pleasure. But it wasn't just his body that burnt for her, hot and fulfilling though their lovemaking had always been. He wanted *her*, his Nell.

He watched a black cat saunter across the car park, stopping for a moment when it noticed him, its green eyes narrowing before it dismissed him as unimportant and continued with its leisurely walk. The cat that walked alone, he thought fancifully. Like Nell. She'd come to the same conclusion about him as that damn animal, whereas he needed her in every part of his life. He wanted to share waking up together at the weekend and reading the Sunday papers in bed while they ate croissants and drank coffee, watching TV with a glass of wine after a hard day's work while the dinner cooked, going to the theatre or to a film, or simply taking a long walk in the evening arm in arm. In the early days they'd done all those things and they had talked about anything and everything—or so he'd thought. Now he realised there was a huge part of her psyche she'd kept from him.

He started the car, frowning to himself.

He'd known she'd been damaged by her earlier life when he'd got to know her, of course. He'd just underestimated the extent of the damage and that had been fatal. Or maybe his ego had ridden roughshod over any concerns he might have had, telling him he would be able to deal with any difficulties in the future.

He nosed the powerful car out of the car park and onto the road beyond, deep in thought. But all that was relative now. One thing was for sure, she wouldn't have responded to him as she'd done last night if she didn't still care for him, deep down somewhere. And when he'd asked her if she loved him she hadn't said no. Admittedly, she hadn't said yes either...

He'd call her tonight, as she'd suggested. Everything in him wanted to come back here and bang on the door till she let him in so he could convince her how much he loved her, but something told him that would accomplish nothing. He'd played the waiting game for months, hadn't he? He could play it a little longer. But this time on his terms. She wouldn't go back on her word, she'd work at Hillview and he knew how fond she was of his mother. That was the reason he'd suggested this in the first place.

Well, he conceded in the next moment. Not the only reason. It was true his mother's heart wasn't good since the hip operation but she hadn't been quite so...difficult about the garden as he'd led Melanie to believe. But Hillview's grounds *did* need a complete overhaul and his mother, albeit with a very pointed glance at his and Melanie's wedding portrait, which still kept pride of place over the mantelpiece in her sitting room, *had* said she wouldn't allow a stranger in to do the work. He knew his mother was with him one hundred per cent; she'd loved Melanie like a daughter and grieved for her daily.

He'd drive back to the house, shower and change his clothes, and go to the office after a pot of strong black coffee, and ring Melanie tonight. And he had no intention of fooling himself the road to getting her back was going to be easy, he just knew it was a road he'd keep walking until... He shook his head. There was no until. He'd walk it. End of story.

CHAPTER FOUR

IT HADN'T been a particularly exhausting day, not compared to some, but when Melanie walked into the cottage that evening she felt bone-weary. Try as she might she'd been unable to think of anything else but Forde all day, endless post-mortems addling her brain until she barely knew which end of her was up. If James had asked her once if she was OK, he'd asked her a dozen times. She wondered what her very able assistant would have said if she'd told him she was verging on a cataclysmic nervous breakdown, she thought wryly, going through the nightly routine of taking off her boots on the mat and then heading for the stairs. Laughed, most likely, because he wouldn't have taken her seriously. James thought she was the ultimate cool, collected, modern woman. Everyone did. Only Forde had ever understood the real her.

She mentally slapped herself for the thought. None of that. If she was going to take up the threads of this new life again—threads that had nearly been broken last night—then she had to control her mind. Simple. Only it wasn't.

After turning on the taps for a warm bath, she went through to the bedroom, steeling herself to glance at the bed. It was rumpled and very, very empty. A shaft of physical pain made her wince. Grimly, she stripped off the covers and dumped them in her linen basket for a wash, opening the windows wide to let in the perfumed night air. It was her imagination that she could still smell Forde's unique scent—a mixture of the expensive aftershave he favoured and his own chemical make-up, which turned into an intoxicating fragrance on his male skin.

It was as she was slipping off her jeans that she noticed the little ball of paper in a corner of the room where it had clearly been thrown. Her note. Oh, Forde, Forde…

She shut her eyes for a moment but tears still seeped beneath her closed lids. What must he have felt like reading it? But she couldn't go there. She mustn't. Walking across the room, she bent and picked it up. She didn't straighten the paper out but held the little ball in one hand, stroking where he'd touched with one finger, guilt and shame washing over her.

She continued to cry all the time she was in the bath, but after she'd washed her hair and dried herself, she splashed her hot face with cold water and took stock. No more crying. She was done.

She pulled on an old pair of comfortable cotton pyjamas and looped her damp hair into a high bun, before going downstairs and fixing herself something to eat with the groceries she'd collected on the way home. It was hard to force the food down; she was on tenterhooks waiting for Forde's call, but she managed to clear her plate and her full stomach helped to quieten her jangling nerves some.

The call came at eight o'clock.

'Hi.' His voice was cool and steady. She expected him to ask how she was or mention her ignominious flight before he awoke that morning, but, Forde being Forde, he didn't do the expected. 'We need to iron out the details for you to work at Hillview. You said you had some conditions?'

'Yes.' Her voice came out as a squeak and she cleared her throat. His rich, smoky tones had brought a whole rush of emotions she could have done without. 'But before I start, are you sure Isabelle will want me around after—after everything?'

'After you walking out and demanding a divorce, you mean?' His even voice belied the content of his words. 'Quite sure. My mother has always taken the view that what goes on between a couple is their business and theirs alone. You know her, you should realise that. Now, your conditions?'

Melanie felt she'd been thoroughly put in her place, and her voice was crisp when she said, 'Firstly, in spite of what you've just said, I shall need to come and see Isabelle and discuss whether she wants me to do the job. If she does, then I'll take it, but all the arrangements will be between myself and your mother. I don't want you involved.'

'Can you see my mother letting me be involved?' he asked drily.

'What I mean is—'

'What you mean is that you don't want me around, popping in for a visit, things like that?'

It was exactly what she meant. 'I can't stop you visiting your mother,' she prevaricated awkwardly, 'but in the circumstances it would be better all round if you tried to avoid doing so when I'm there, I guess.'

'Noted.'

Oh, hell, this was going worse than she'd imagined. 'Of course if there's a crisis of some kind with Isabelle's health—'

'I'll be allowed on the premises,' he finished for her.

'Look, Forde—'

'Next condition,' he said politely.

Melanie took a deep breath. She was *not* going to let him get under her skin. 'James and I are working on a job at the moment and there's another lined up straight afterwards, which cannot wait, but it won't take long. We were due to begin a fairly substantial project mid-September but I've been in touch with the people concerned and they're happy to delay a while. In fact they've said they'd prefer the work doing in the spring because—' She faltered; too late she wished she hadn't begun the sentence. 'Because the lady is expecting a baby at the end of October and hasn't been too well lately. Her husband feels it would have been a little stressful for her. So, we've a space for Isabelle if she wants it.'

'Business is good by the sound of it.'

She swallowed hard. 'Yes, yes, it is.'

'One thing I must make clear, and this isn't to be shared with my mother. I intend to pay for the work, my Christmas present to her, but as she's somewhat proud at the best of times I shan't mention it until the job is finished. With that in mind, there will be no need to worry about getting anything but the best in materials and so on, but you might like to quote her a substantially lower price than is realistic. Once you've priced the job and given me an estimate, you have my word I will pay in full whenever you wish. Understood?'

She took a moment to consider his words. She *had* intended to do the work at the very lowest margin she could manage, but if Forde was paying it would mean she could price it the same way she would do for anyone else. And she could understand why Forde was keeping it a secret until it was a fait accompli. Isabelle was extraordinarily proud of her successful son but had always refused to accept a penny from him, declaring Forde's father's death had left her mortgage free and with a nest egg in the form of a life assurance her husband had taken out some years before he'd died. Having had Forde late in life at the age of forty-three, Isabelle also had a very good pension from the civil service where she'd been employed all her working life before leaving to become a full-time mother when Forde was born.

Melanie cleared her throat. 'I understand. It might be helpful to me if payment for the bulk of the materials I use could be given as the job progresses. Cash flow and so on.'

'Fine. When can you talk to her?'

'Tomorrow evening?' Better to get it over with.

'Good. I'll ring her tonight and tell her I've suggested you for the work and you're agreeable, depending on the job when you assess it, and you'll be in contact tomorrow. OK? Anything else?' he added crisply.

It was totally unfair, not to mention perverse, but his businesslike tone was making her want to scream. Last night they'd indulged in wild, abandoned sex and she'd slept in his arms, and he was talking as though he were discussing a contract with some colleague or other. Keeping her voice as devoid of emotion as his, Melanie said, 'I don't think so at this stage.'

'Goodnight, then.' And the phone went dead.

Melanie stared blankly across the room. 'You pig.' But at least she didn't feel like crying any more. Throwing something, yes, but not crying.

Isabelle picked up the phone on the second ring the next evening, and was as gentle and courteous as she'd always been. So it was, promptly at two o'clock the following Sunday afternoon, normally her housework and catch-up day, Melanie presented herself at Forde's mother's fine Victorian house situated some ten miles or so from the home she and Forde had shared.

She was so nervous she was trembling as she rang the bell, but it was a uniformed nurse who opened the door rather than Isabelle. The woman showed her into Isabelle's comfortable sitting room where a wood fire crackled in the grate despite the warm weather, for all the world as though she were a stranger rather than her patient's daughter-in-law, which led Melanie to believe the nurse wasn't aware she was Forde's wife.

Isabelle confirmed this the moment the nurse had shut the door, leaving them alone. 'Hello, my dear.' Forde's mother was sitting on a sofa pulled close to the fire and she lifted up her face for Melanie to kiss her cheek as she'd always done in the past, before patting the seat beside her. 'Sit down. I didn't tell Nurse Bannister who you were. She's a nosy soul and always poking her nose into this and that. Thank heaven she'll be leaving at the end of next week and not a day too soon. I can't wait to have my house back to myself.'

'Hello, Isabelle.' Melanie's voice was shaky. She'd half expected Forde's mother to look ill and pale, for things to be different somehow, but instead both Isabelle and this room were exactly the same. She had left Forde, then left the city and made a new life for herself, but it was as though the last seven months had never happened and she had been here the day before. The same floor-to-ceiling bookshelves lined with books graced two walls of the somewhat old-fashioned room, the same heavily patterned wool carpet covering the floor and thick embossed drapes at the window... She took a deep breath. 'How are you? Forde told me you've been in hospital recently.' She'd decided to mention his name straight away rather than having him hanging over the proceedings like a spectre at the feast.

Isabelle smiled. 'I was foolish enough to break a hip and then my heart played up a little, but what can you expect at my age? I'm no spring chicken. More to the point, how are *you*, dear?'

'Very well, thank you.' Telling herself she had to say what she'd rehearsed for days, Melanie took the plunge. 'Isabelle, when I returned your letter it wasn't because I didn't want to keep in touch, not really, but because I—I couldn't.'

A pair of silvery-blue eyes very like Forde's smiled at her. 'I know that, dear. It had to be a clean sweep for you to be able to go on. We were too fond of each other for it to be any different.'

She wanted to cry. She wanted to lay her head on Isabelle's lap and cry and cry, as she had done the first time she'd seen Forde's mother after losing Matthew. Isabelle had cried with her then, telling her she would never forget Matthew but there would be other babies to take away the edge of her grief and loss. Frightened by the way she was feeling, Melanie retreated. 'You want the garden replanning, I understand.'

Isabelle accepted the change of conversation with her normal grace. '*Want* is perhaps not the right word. *Need* is better. I have to confess it's become a little too much lately.'

'And you don't want a gardener in to see to things?'

'Occasionally, but not every day. As you know I've put in several hours most days for years—it's my pleasure. I can still do a little but not all that's required.'

'So if we got it under control, my assistant coming in perhaps once a month for a couple of days wouldn't distress you too much?' Melanie asked gently, feeling for Forde's mother. The grounds were beautiful and they'd been Isabelle's pride and joy. 'You'll like James,' she added. 'I promise.'

'I'm sure I will. Now, Nurse Bannister is bringing us a cup of tea and then I thought we might see the garden together?'

Melanie nodded. In truth she wanted to get out of this room. She had noticed at once that Isabelle had kept their wedding picture in its elaborate gold frame exactly where it had always been, and she'd avoided looking at it since. The tall, dark, smiling man and his radiant bride could have been different people, so far removed did she feel from the girl in the photograph.

It was clear Nurse Bannister had made the connection when she returned with the tray of tea a few moments later, her gimlet-hard eyes searching Melanie's face avidly. With no trouble Melanie decided she could quite understand Isabelle's desire to be rid of the companion Forde—for all the right reasons, of course—had thrust upon his mother.

By the time she left Hillview three hours later Melanie felt she had a good idea of what Isabelle would like, and more importantly *not* like, in the new garden. They'd agreed to leave well alone where they could and all the mature trees would remain, but Melanie had encouraged Isabelle to treat the acre of ground as a series of compartments flowing into and round each other to create a whole. Easy maintenance being the prime concern, Melanie had suggested vigorous ground cover in places, evergreen, naturally dense plants planted to form a thatch of vegetation that would give weeds little opportunity to develop. A water feature in the form of a large sunken pool surrounded by a pebble 'beach' to keep down weeds and an area for sitting in one part of the garden, in another a landscaped rockery with helianthemums, verbascums and sisyrinchiums to give vibrant colour, a bed of gravel aiding drainage and avoiding waterlogging.

Isabelle had listened to all her suggestions, welcoming the idea of winding paths leading to arbours and two or three patio areas, along with several chamomile lawns. This aromatic perennial would provide a contrast of texture to other areas of the garden, and when bruised by light treading the leaves would release a pleasant apple-like scent. The main advantage over a grass lawn for Isabelle was that the chamomile only would need very occasional trimming, which James could see to.

An area of decking surrounded by scented shrubs; a sunny, gentle slope adapted to suit sun-loving plants chosen for their rich flowering and compact shape on a bed of tiny, different-coloured pebbles; dramatic island beds of large shrubs surrounded by lavender or ornamental grasses—Melanie had come up with them all, and Isabelle had been remarkably open to the changes.

They had agreed Melanie would go away and make scale drawings recording features of both the present garden and the new proposed changes, so that Isabelle could review the options and make sure she was completely happy. Melanie had told her mother-in-law that, at the initial stage, Isabelle must treat the drawing as a base plan and she could use overlays of tracing paper to test out different ideas. Once Isabelle was sure how she wanted the changes to look, Melanie would make detailed planting plans for particular areas as well as drawing up cross-sections of specific features, like the pool, the arbour and grass walk they'd discussed, the topiary and other ideas. Nothing was definite and Isabelle had the right to change her mind as many times as she wanted to, Melanie had impressed on the old lady, knowing it was a little overwhelming for her.

They parted with a kiss and a hug, Isabelle holding her tight for a little longer than was strictly necessary. Melanie had a lump in her throat as she drove away from the house. It had felt so *right* to be with Isabelle again, but she didn't dwell on her feelings, applying her mind to the drawings she would make on graph paper from her notes and thinking of one or two other ideas as she drove. Softening the stone walls surrounding a patio area by planting vibrant flowers and trailing plants in the top of it, and maybe staggered railway sleepers in the far corner to give a step effect with boulders and varied plants.

She wanted Isabelle's garden to continue to be a sanctuary to be enjoyed by the old lady, a retreat from the world, and to that end she was planning paths that curled from one feature to another, shady corners with trees and shrubs and sunny spots like the rockery and pool. And lots of benches, comfortable wooden ones, she told herself, where Isabelle could sit and rest any time anywhere in the grounds.

The changes were going to take a lot of money but there was no reason why, at the end of it all, Isabelle's original high-maintenance garden, which had always been kept in a state of perfection by the dedicated gardener her mother-in-law had been, couldn't be turned into something just as beautiful but dramatically more labour friendly. In fact she would make sure of it, Melanie determined.

Once home, she made a pot of coffee and began work at the dining table. She was deep into transferring all the measurements she'd taken that afternoon onto her rough plan when the phone rang. Her mind occupied with right angles and base lines and boundaries, she lifted up the receiver and spoke automatically. 'Hello, Melanie Masterson.'

'Hello, Melanie Masterson. This is Forde Masterson speaking.'

Her heart ricocheted off her ribcage and then galloped at twice its speed. Somehow she managed to say fairly normally, 'Oh, hi, Forde. I was working.'

'I won't keep you,' he said, the faintly teasing note that had been in his voice disappearing.

She wanted to say it was OK, that she hadn't meant it like that, as a put-down, but, telling herself it was better to keep things businesslike and formal, she kept quiet.

'I just called to thank you for how you handled my mother. She phoned a while ago and, from being more than a little apprehensive about her beloved garden being chopped about, as she'd put it initially, she came across as actually excited about the changes you'd discussed. I appreciate it, Nell.'

As ever, hearing the special nickname sent a flicker of desire sizzling along her nerve endings. His power over her was absolute, she recognised with a stab of dismay. Nothing had changed. Just hearing his voice made her want him so badly she was trembling with it.

'Nell? Are you still there?'

'Yes, I'm here,' she said quickly, pulling herself together. 'And there's no need to thank me. You do realise it's going to be pretty expensive if we do it properly.'

'Of course.' There was a pause. 'Would it be crass to point out you know what I'm worth and money isn't a consideration? I just want her satisfied at the end of it.'

'She will be.' Melanie found she didn't want him to finish the conversation. She wanted to keep talking to him, hearing those deep, smoky tones. She should never have agreed to do the job, she thought as fear at her vulnerability where Forde was concerned streaked through her. This was crazy, just asking for trouble. 'She'll love it, Forde. I promise.'

'I don't doubt that for a moment,' he said softly. 'I trust you, Nell. I always have.'

Panic gave her the strength to say, 'I have to go now. I'll be in touch once Isabelle's decided exactly what she wants and I've planned and costed everything. Goodbye, Forde.'

'Goodnight, sweetheart. Sweet dreams.'

He'd put the phone down before her stunned mind could compute again. *Sweetheart?* And sweet dreams? What had happened to her conditions? she thought frantically as she went into the kitchen to fix more coffee, needing its boost to calm her shattered nerves. Admittedly she hadn't actually spelled out 'no endearments,' but surely he'd got the message?

She found he had completely ruined her concentration when she tried to work on the drawings again. Eventually she took an aspirin for the pounding headache that had developed in the last hour or so and went to bed, there to toss and turn half the night, and have X-rated dreams in which Forde rated highly for the other half.

Nevertheless, when she awoke early Monday morning her steely resolve was back. The divorce was going through, come hell or high water, she determined as she sat eating her breakfast in the tiny courtyard, feeling like a wet rag. Absolutely nothing could prevent it. *Nothing.* It was the only way she could ever regain some peace of mind again.

CHAPTER FIVE

CONTRARY to what Melanie had expected after Forde's call the day she had visited his mother, the next four weeks passed by without further contact with him. She visited Isabelle twice more during the time she was finishing the other contracts, and they ironed out exactly what was required to their mutual satisfaction.

On her second visit, Melanie took James along with her. He was fully acquainted with the circumstances but—James-like—had taken it all in his stride as though it were the most natural thing in the world for an estranged wife who was seeking a divorce to undertake a major job for her mother-in-law.

Melanie could tell Isabelle was a little taken aback at first when she met James. He *was* something of an Adonis with a smile that could charm the birds out of the trees, but, just so her mother-in-law didn't put two and two together and make ten, she took her aside at one point when James was busy measuring this and that at the other end of the garden and made it clear theirs was a working relationship and nothing more.

'Of course, dear,' Isabelle said sweetly, as though the thought of anything else hadn't crossed her mind, but Melanie noticed her mother-in-law's smile was warmer the next time she conversed with James. For his part, James was his normal, sunny self and by the end of the afternoon he had Isabelle eating out of his hand, which boded well for the future.

The night before they were due to start work at Hillview, Melanie didn't sleep well. The August heatwave had continued into an Indian summer, and it was even hotter in September if anything. Everywhere, the ground was baked dry, and, although this was slightly preferable to working in drenching rain and mud, it wasn't ideal. But it wasn't the pending job that had her giving up all thought of further sleep at four in the morning and going downstairs to make a pot of coffee, which she took outside into the courtyard; it was Forde.

There had scarcely been a waking minute he hadn't invaded her thoughts since the night they'd slept together, and even when she'd fallen asleep he was still there, carving his place in her subconscious. *And she hadn't heard from him.* Not a word. Not a phone call. Nothing. She'd submitted a ridiculously low estimate to Isabelle as he had requested once she'd worked out the pricing of the job, and a realistic one to him via his office rather than his home, thinking this emphasised the businesslike nature of the arrangement. His secretary had called the next day to say that Mr Masterson was happy with the estimate and his confirmation of acceptance would arrive by return of post. Which it had. A signature in the required space. Great.

Melanie wrinkled her nose in the scented darkness. He'd finally cut his losses and moved on, that was plain to see. The last ridiculous scenario when she'd all but begged him to make love to her and then frozen him out the next morning had been too much. She didn't blame him. How could she? Why would any man put his hand up to take on a nutcase like her? And it was what was necessary, what she'd been aiming for, so why did it feel as though her heart were being torn out by its roots?

She sighed heavily, swigging back half a cup of coffee and looking up into the dark velvet sky above, punctured by hundreds of twinkling stars. She had to get a handle on this. Her dream of a happy-ever-after ending had been smashed to pieces months ago so why was she dredging up the past? She wasn't like anyone else—that was what Forde didn't understand. And it wasn't his fault he'd married a jinxed woman. But she would never let herself get close to anyone again; that way she couldn't be hurt and neither could anyone else.

Finishing the last of the coffee, she continued to sit on as the sky lightened and the birds woke up, her limbs leaden. She hadn't really slept well since Forde had come back into her life again—not that he'd ever left, if she was being brutally honest. She might not have spoken to or seen him those seven months before he had written to her, but he'd only been a heartbeat away, nonetheless.

This had to get better, she told herself miserably. It must. She couldn't spend the rest of her life feeling like this. Her grief and remorse about Matthew would always be with her; she had come to terms with that and in a strange way almost welcomed it. If she couldn't do anything else for her darling little boy she could mourn him, and as long as she was alive he would never be forgotten but cherished in her heart. But the sense of loss about Forde was different and much more complicated.

Stop analysing. She shut her eyes, letting the first gentle rays of the sun warm her face. By ten or eleven o'clock it would be baking hot and less of a blessing, but right now it felt comforting. She felt so tired—physically, mentally and emotionally—but she had to keep going. And there were people so much worse off than she was: folk with terminal illnesses or severe health issues. At least she was young and strong and fit. She mustn't turn into a whinger—she'd always hated them.

The silent pep talk helped a little, enough to get her on her feet anyway. After leaving the coffee tray in the kitchen she went upstairs to shower and change, and by seven o'clock was on the road. After picking James up from the house he rented with three friends—it was pointless them both driving the hundred-mile round trip each day—they drove to Hillview on roads not yet traffic logged with morning traffic, arriving at Isabelle's house just after eight.

The first thing Melanie noticed was Forde's Aston Martin parked in the driveway. Her stomach somersaulted, but James was unfurling himself out of the truck and stretching, and didn't glance at her before starting to unload some of the equipment in the back of the pickup. By the time she joined him on the drive she was in command of herself, but angry. Forde had *promised* he'd stay away when she was around, and she didn't believe for a moment he wasn't aware she was starting work today. This was so, so unfair.

She heard the front door open and knew by some sixth sense Forde was standing there, but she didn't glance his way, continuing to help James until they were done. By that time Forde had walked down the drive from the house to where they were parked, some yards from the Aston Martin.

'Good morning.' His voice was cool, clipped, and as she looked at him she saw the silver-blue eyes were cold and he wasn't smiling.

Her anger went up a notch. How dared he look at her like that when he shouldn't be here? Her tone matching his, she said pointedly, 'Good morning, Forde. I'm starting work on the garden today or had it slipped your memory?'

'No, it hadn't slipped my memory,' he said evenly, holding out his hand to James as he added, 'I'm Forde Masterson, Melanie's husband. I take it you're James?'

She'd forgotten she'd employed James after she'd left Forde and the two men hadn't met. She watched James take Forde's hand almost gingerly and she didn't blame him; Forde was making no effort to be friendly, his face straight and his eyes narrowed.

James mumbled a polite hello and then extracted his hand, saying he'd start taking some of the equipment to the back of the house before scampering off with armfuls of tools.

'You spoke about your assistant as though he was a young lad just out of school and wet behind the ears,' Forde said accusingly. 'He's a grown man of what— twenty-four, twenty-five?'

'What?' Why was he talking about James when he knew full well he shouldn't *be* here?

'And he looks to me as though he knows his way about,' Forde added grimly. 'In every sense of the word.'

'James backpacked round the world for three or four years with his friends after leaving uni, and I have never suggested he was a young boy.' Melanie glared at Forde. 'Not that that's any of your business. And why are you here this morning anyway?'

'So I was right. He's twenty-four, twenty-five?'

Why this obsession with James's age? 'He's twenty-six, and, I repeat, why are you here?'

'Answering an early-morning summons by my mother because she thought she had a bird down the chimney,' Forde answered shortly. 'OK? And before you ask, no, there was no damn bird.'

Since an incident some years ago when a large wood pigeon had fallen down Isabelle's chimney and then positioned itself on a ledge a few feet up from the fireplace where it had cooed frantically until Forde had arrived and got it out, along with a cloud of soot and grime that had covered the room in smuts, there had been several such fruitless summonses by Forde's mother. Isabelle lived in horror of inadvertently lighting the fire and burning a bird alive, even though Forde had told her repeatedly that the stainless-steel mesh bird cowl he'd had installed in the top of the chimney to prevent just such a catastrophe made it impossible. When she had still lived with Forde he had been convinced that the wood pigeon he'd rescued took a fiendish delight in sitting on the roof and calling down the chimney to fool his mother and cause him grief.

'Oh.' Melanie nodded, feeling guilty of her suspicions, and—although she would rather die than admit it, even to herself—a little piqued that his presence had absolutely nothing to do with a desire to see her.

'So this James.' Forde raked back his hair with an

impatient hand. 'Is he married? Got a long-term girl-friend? What?'

He was jealous. As the light dawned Melanie stared at him in amazement. He surely didn't think… She didn't know whether to take it as a compliment or an insult that he thought a handsome, virile, young stud like James would bother with a married woman two years older than himself and with enough baggage to fill umpteen football stadiums. She decided on the latter. 'James's personal life is his own business,' she said icily. 'He works for me, that's all, Forde. Got it?'

Forde looked spectacularly unconvinced.

'He favours statuesque brunettes who can play tennis and squash and all the other sports he's mad about as well as he does, and who can stay up all night dancing in clubs and then go sailing after breakfast,' Melanie stated firmly. 'But even if I was his type, and he mine, it still wouldn't be an option. I'm his employer, he's my employee. End of story.'

She watched him expel a silent sigh. It was a completely inopportune moment to feel such a consuming love for him it stopped her breath. She dropped her eyes, scared he might see what he must not see. He clearly hadn't stopped to shave before he'd left home and the black stubble accentuated his rugged good looks tenfold. Combine that with the casual clothes he was wearing—open-necked shirt showing a hint of dark body hair and beautifully cut cotton trousers—and he was any maiden's prayer. Their mother's and grandmother's too.

His voice came low and intense. 'This should be the moment when I say I'm sorry and I have no right to ask, but I'm not sorry and I have every right to ask. You're my wife.'

It was one of the hardest things she'd ever done to raise her gaze to his without betraying herself. 'It's over, Forde.'

'It will never be over,' he said roughly. 'It wasn't a piece of paper that joined us, Nell, or a man of the cloth saying a few words and two gold rings. You're mine, body, soul and spirit. I love you and I know you love me.'

He watched her face as he spoke but all the barriers were up and he couldn't read a thing.

'We can't go back to how it was,' she said with a quietness that was more final than any show of emotion.

'No,' he said softly. 'We can't. We had a son together and he died, and he'll for ever be a part of us and a sadness that's shaped us into the people we are today. But you and I, that is a thing apart. This punishing yourself for something that wasn't your fault has to end.'

'What?' She reared up as though he had slapped her.

'That's what you are doing, Nell, whether you acknowledge it or not, and you're punishing me too,' he said, feeling incredibly cruel to face her with what he believed. But he would lose her if he didn't start to force her to take stock.

'You don't understand anything.'

He flinched visibly, telling himself to keep calm. How she could come out with something like that when all he'd done since Matthew's death *was* understand, he didn't know. 'This is not all about you—have you considered that?' He could hear her damn assistant coming back, whistling some pop tune or other, and wanted—

quite unreasonably—to punch him on the nose. 'I loved Matthew too.'

'But you didn't cause his death.'

'Neither did you, for crying out loud.' He hadn't meant to shout, he'd told himself before he walked out of the house he was going to be calm and rational, but at least the whistling had stopped.

She turned away, her soft mouth pulling tight in a way he knew from past experience meant she was digging her heels in. 'I've work to do.' She glanced up to where James was standing some distance away, clearly uncertain of whether he was welcome in what was obviously a danger zone. 'James, come and help me with the rest of this.'

Knowing if he didn't leave fairly rapidly he was going to say or do something he'd be sorry for, Forde turned on his heel and walked back to the house without another word. His mother was waiting for him in the hall, just inside the open front door.

'I heard you shout.' Isabelle's voice was gently accusing.

He loved his mother. She was a strong-minded, generous soul with the faintly old-world charm and dignity of her generation, and for that reason he bit back the profanities hovering on his tongue and said curtly, 'It was that or strangle her, so be thankful for the shouting.'

Isabelle's eyes widened. She opened her mouth to say something and then clearly thought better of it.

'I'm going.' Forde bent and kissed her forehead. 'I'll ring you later.'

When he left the house again Melanie and James were nowhere to be seen, although he could hear voices beyond the stone wall that separated the drive and the front of the house from the gardens at the rear. He glanced at the side gate for a moment and then decided there was nothing to be gained from saying goodbye. Striding over to the Aston Martin, he opened the door and slid inside, starting the car immediately and swinging it round so fast the tyres screeched.

That hadn't gone at all as he'd intended, he thought, gripping the steering wheel so hard his knuckles showed white. He hadn't expected her assistant to look like a young George Clooney with muscles for one thing, or for Melanie to be so... He couldn't find a word that satisfactorily described her mix of cool hauteur and wariness and gave up trying.

Once he'd reached home he prowled round the house like a restless animal instead of showering and getting changed for the office. Everywhere he looked there were reminders of Melanie; she'd so enjoyed having the team of interior designers in when they'd first got married and stamping her mark on the house. And he loved her taste. In fact he loved everything about her, damn it, although there had been moments after she had left him when the pain had got so bad he'd wished he'd never met her.

He had never imagined there would be a problem in life where he couldn't reach her, that was the thing. He'd been confident whatever befell them he'd be able to protect and nurture her, see her through, that they would face it together. But he had been wrong. And it had cost him his marriage. He walked through to the massive kitchen-cum-breakfast-room at the back of the house and slumped down at the kitchen table.

He was still deep in black thoughts when Janet let herself into the house at gone ten.

'Mr Masterson, what are you doing here at this time in the morning?' She had always insisted on giving him his full title even though he'd told her to call him Forde a hundred times. 'Are you ill?'

He lifted bleak eyes to the round, robin-like ones of the little woman who was a friend and confidante as much as his cook and cleaner. Janet's life was far from easy but you'd never have guessed it from her bright and cheery manner, and in the ten years she'd worked for him since he had first bought the house they'd grown close. She was a motherly soul, and he looked on her as the older sister he'd never had. For her part, he knew she regarded him like one of her sons and she had never been backward in admonishing him, should the situation call for it. He could tell Janet anything, unlike his mother. Not that Isabelle wouldn't have understood or given good advice, but since his father's death he'd always felt he had to shield his mother from problems and worry.

'I saw Melanie this morning,' he said flatly. 'It wasn't an…amicable exchange.'

'Oh, dear.' Janet bustled over to the coffee maker and put it on. 'Have you eaten yet?'

He shook his head.

Once he had a mug of steaming coffee and a plateful of egg and bacon inside him, he felt a little better. Pouring him a second cup and one for herself, Janet plonked herself opposite him at the kitchen table. 'So,' she said companionably. 'What happened?'

He told her the gist of the conversation and Janet listened quietly. After a moment, she said, 'So you think Mrs Masterson is having an affair with her assistant?'

Forde straightened as suddenly as though he'd had an electric shock. 'Of course not.'

'But you're going to give up on her, nonetheless?'

'Of course not,' he said again, getting angry. 'You know me better than that, Janet.'

'Then why are you sitting here moping?' Janet said, giving him one of her straight looks.

The penny dropped and Forde smiled sheepishly. 'Right.'

'I told you when she left like that it was going to be a long job and you needed to be patient as well as persistent, now didn't I?' Janet poured them both more coffee. 'The way she was that day before the ambulance came, it was more than the normal shock and despair someone would feel in the same circumstances. Mrs Masterson really believes there's some sort of jinx on her that touches those close to her.'

Forde stared at her. Janet had mentioned this before but he hadn't given it much credence, thinking that Melanie was too sensible to really believe such nonsense. 'But that's rubbish.'

'You know that and I know it,' Janet said stoutly, 'but as for Mrs Masterson...'

Forde leant back in his chair, his eyes narrowed. 'She's an intelligent, enlightened, astute young woman, for goodness' sake. I don't think—'

'She's a young wife who lost her first baby in a terrible accident and she blames herself totally. Add that to what I've just said, bearing in mind the facts about her parents, grandmother and even a friend at school she mentioned to me, all of whom were taken away from her, and reconsider, Mr Masterson. Melanie had a miserable childhood and became accustomed to keeping everything deep inside her and presenting a façade to the rest of the world. It doesn't come natural for her to speak about her feelings, not even to you. And, begging your pardon, don't forget you're a man. Your sex work on logic and common sense.'

Forde looked down at the gold band on the third finger of his left hand. 'Let me get this right. You're saying she thinks if she'd stayed with me something would happen to me?'

'Mrs Masterson probably wouldn't be able to put it into words but, yes, that is what I think. And there's an element of punishing herself too, the why-should-I-be-happy-after-what-I've-done syndrome.' Janet shrugged. 'In its own way, it's perfectly understandable.'

Forde stared at her. 'Hell,' he said.

'Quite.' Janet nodded briskly. 'So you save her from herself.'

'How?' he said a trifle desperately. 'Exactly how, Janet?'

Janet stood up and began to clear the table. 'Now that I don't know, but you'll find a way, loving her like you do.'

Forde smiled wryly. 'And here was I thinking you had all the answers.'

'She loves you very much, Mr Masterson, that's what you have to remember. It's her Achilles' heel.'

'You really think that? That she still loves me?'

Janet smiled at the man she had come to think of as one of her own brood. As big and as tough as he was, Mr Masterson had a real soft centre and that was what she liked best about him. Some men with his wealth and looks would think they were God's gift to womankind, but not Mr Masterson. She didn't think he wasn't ruthless when it was necessary, mind, but then he wouldn't have got to where he was now without a bit of steel in his make-up. 'Sure she loves you,' she said softly. 'Like you love her. And love always finds a way. You remember that when you're feeling like you did this morning.' She wagged a finger at him. 'All right?'

Forde got up, his silver-blue eyes holding a warmth that would have amazed his business rivals. 'You're a treasure, Janet. What would I do without you?'

'That's what my hubby always says when he rolls back from the pub after one too many,' Janet said drily, 'usually after helping himself to what's in my purse.'

'You're too good for him. You know that, don't you?'

Janet smiled at him as Forde left the kitchen. Be that as it may, and she certainly didn't disagree with Forde's summing up of her Geoff, Mr and Mrs Masterson were a perfect match. She had always thought so.

Her smile faded. She just hoped they could work their problems out, that was all. In spite of her encouraging words to Mr Masterson, she was worried Mrs Masterson would never come home, short of a miracle.

CHAPTER SIX

IT WAS the middle of November. A mild November, thus far, with none of the heavy frosts and icy temperatures that could make working outside difficult. But Melanie wasn't thinking of the weather as she left the doctor's surgery. She walked over to her pickup truck in the car park, but once she was sitting inside she didn't start the engine, staring blindly out of the windscreen.

She hadn't seen Forde since the day she had begun working for Isabelle, although he had phoned her several times, ostensibly with questions about his mother's garden. On learning from her solicitor that they'd been waiting for some time for Forde to sign and return certain documents appertaining to the divorce, she'd called *him* at home two nights ago.

She leant back in the truck's old, tattered seat and shut her eyes. Forde had been cheerfully apologetic about the delay, making some excuse about pressure of work, but what had really got under her skin was the woman's voice she'd heard in the background when she'd been talking to him. She hadn't asked him who he was with, she had no right whatsoever to question him after the way she'd walked out of their home and the marriage, but it had hurt her more than she would have thought possible to think of another woman in their home.

Stupid. Opening her eyes, she inhaled deeply. Forde was at liberty to see whomever he wished. Nevertheless, she hadn't been able to sleep that night. She had arrived at work the next morning feeling ill, and when she'd fainted clean away as she and James had been preparing a gravelled area for a number of architectural and structural plants her assistant had been scared to death.

Poor James. If she weren't so shocked and dazed at what the doctor had found she could have smiled. He'd been beside himself, saying she hadn't been well for weeks and what if she fainted again when she was driving or using some of the equipment they'd hired for the job? She could badly injure herself or worse. In the end, just to appease him, she had promised to call her doctor's surgery and as it happened they'd had a cancellation this morning. She had walked into Dr Chisholm's room explaining she knew she was suffering from stress and all her symptoms could be put down to that, and if she could just have some pills to take the edge off she would be fine. He'd gently reminded her that *he* was the doctor and he'd prefer to give her a thorough examination after asking her a few questions.

Her hands trembling, she forced herself to start the engine. She had to get back to work. There was still plenty to do at Hillview and each day the mild weather continued was a bonus. The old-timers were predicting that a mild October and November meant the country would suffer for it come December and January. They were on target to finish the job mid-December and if any bad weather could hold off till then, it would be a huge benefit.

But she found she couldn't drive. She was shaking too much. She sat huddled in her seat as reality began to dawn on her stunned mind. She was expecting a baby. Forde's baby. That one night in August had had repercussions the like of which she hadn't imagined in her wildest dreams. With hindsight, it was ridiculous she hadn't suspected the non-appearance of her monthlies, the tiredness and queasiness that had developed into bouts of nausea and sickness could be something other than stress. But she hadn't. She really hadn't. Perhaps she'd blanked her mind to the possibility she could be pregnant, but there was no mistaking it now. She was *thirteen weeks* pregnant.

She had fainted a couple of times in the early days when she was carrying Matthew. *Matthew.* Oh, Matthew, Matthew... She began to cry, her mind in turmoil. 'I'm sorry, my precious baby,' she murmured helplessly. 'I never meant for this to happen. I love you, I'll always love you. You know that, don't you?'

How long she sat there she didn't know. She only came to herself when her driver's door was suddenly yanked open and Forde crouched down beside her, his voice agonised as he said, 'Nell? Nell, what is it? What's the matter?'

He was the only person she wanted to see and yet the last person, and she couldn't explain that even to herself. Desperately trying to control herself, she stammered, 'Wh-what are you—you doing here?'

He had closed her door and walked round the bonnet, sliding into the passenger seat and taking her into his arms—in spite of the gear stick—before she knew what was happening. 'My mother realised you weren't with James this morning and asked where you were,' he murmured above her head. 'James said you'd gone to the doctor's, that he was worried about you. Damn it, Nell, I'm your husband. If anyone has the right to be worried about you, it's me. What's wrong?'

She hadn't had time to think about this, to decide what to tell him—if anything. But no, she would have to tell him, she thought in the next moment. He had a right to know. He was the father. *The father.* Oh, hell, hell, this couldn't be happening. And yet in spite of her desperate confusion and the feeling she'd let Matthew down in some way, her maternal instincts had risen with a fierceness that had overwhelmed her.

She thought of all the heavy work she'd done over the past weeks and breathed a silent prayer of thankfulness she hadn't lost this tiny person growing inside her. But now she was scared, *petrified* something would happen to the baby because of her.

'Nell?' Forde's voice was a rumble above her head as he continued to hold her close. 'Whatever this is, whatever's wrong, we'll get through it, OK?'

His words acted like an injection of adrenaline. She pulled away, wiping her eyes with the back of her hand in a childish gesture that belied her words when she said baldly, 'I'm pregnant.'

Forde heard the words but for a moment they didn't register. Since his mother had called him to say Melanie was at the doctor's surgery, that she had been ill for weeks without telling anyone, he'd imagined she was suffering from every terminal illness under the sun.

She had been so thin and fragile-looking the last time he'd seen her, he'd told himself with savage self-condemnation. He should have done something about it. And everyone knew certain diseases and conditions were only successfully treated if you did something about them fast. And it had been weeks, months...

He had driven like a madman to the address of the surgery James had given his mother, one eye on every vehicle coming in the opposite direction in case she had passed him. He'd fully expected she would be gone when he pulled into the doctor's car park and when he'd seen the truck had known a moment's deep relief before he'd realised she was bent over the steering wheel with her head in her hands. Then he'd known a panic he'd never felt before.

His face as stunned as hers had been when Dr Chisholm had given her the news, he said, 'What did you say?'

'I'm—I'm expecting a baby.' Drawing on every scrap of composure at her disposal, she went on, 'The night you came to my cottage in August, it happened then. I'm thirteen weeks pregnant.'

He raked back his hair in the old familiar way. 'But you're on the pill.' It had been one of the things they had argued about in the months following the miscarriage, her insistence that she go on the pill to avoid another pregnancy. He'd been patient at first, understanding her mind as well as her body needed time to get over what had happened, but then after one particularly painful row she had told him she didn't want more children, not ever. And that night he had returned to the house to find her gone.

'After I'd left there was no need to take it,' she said flatly.

He stared at her. There hadn't been much need before she'd left; she had hardly let him near her, even to kiss her. She had withdrawn into herself with a completeness that had baffled him. She still baffled him, but... The wonder began to dawn on him. She was *pregnant*. Pregnant with their baby.

As his face lit up Melanie strained away from him, her back pressing against the driver's door. 'No,' she mumbled, fear in her voice as well as her body language. 'I don't want this—can't you see? This doesn't change anything between us.'

'Are you crazy?' he said huskily. 'Of course it does.' And then, as her words hit home, his eyes widened. 'You're not considering a termination?'

Hurt beyond measure he could think such a thing, she felt anger replace panic. 'Of course I'm not,' she all but spat at him. 'I can't believe you said that.'

There was a stark silence as she watched his face change. 'Let me get this right. You want the baby but you don't want me? Is that what you're trying to say?'

Her face white, Melanie shook her head. 'I don't mean that.'

'Then what the hell *do* you mean?' Knowing his voice had been too loud and struggling for calmness, Forde took a rasping breath. 'Look, let's get out of here and go somewhere for a coffee where we can discuss this.'

'*No.*'

It was immediate and again the note of fear was there. Forde could feel his control slipping. She was making him feel like some sort of monster, for crying out loud. She was his wife and this was his baby, and she wouldn't even talk to him?

Whether Melanie realised what he was thinking, he didn't know, but in the next instant he saw her take a deep breath before she said, 'I'm sorry, Forde, really, but I have to have time to adjust to this myself and I need to get back to work—'

'The hell you are.' His face darkened. 'You're thirteen weeks pregnant, woman. Think of the baby.'

Baby. Just the sound of the word brought such a rush of emotion she felt dizzy. 'Women the world over work when they are pregnant,' she pointed out with a calmness she was far from feeling, 'and I shall explain the situation to James and tell him I won't be doing any lifting or carrying of heavy bags and things. But I still need to work, Forde. I *want* to work.'

'You're not well enough,' he said stubbornly.

'Now I know why I've been feeling the way I have I can eat little and often and make sure I don't miss meals or get too tired, but normal life *will* continue.' Feeling a compromise was in order, she added, 'I'll phone you tonight, I promise.'

'Not good enough. I want to sit down with you and discuss this properly. You're carrying my child, Nell. I'll take you out for a meal tonight. Be ready about eight.'

She really didn't want to do this. For one thing the complaint she now recognised was morning sickness tended to be more afternoon and evening sickness, and for another being with Forde was painful at the best of times, reminding her of all she'd lost. 'I don't think—'

She found her words cut off as his mouth took hers.

The kiss was a deliberate assault on her senses, she recognised that from the moment his mouth descended, but he'd taken her by surprise and by the time reason was back she was trembling at the sweetness of his lovemaking. He had moved to lean over her, using one hand to steady himself and the other to lightly cup her breast, but immediately his tongue had slid along her teeth and he had probed her lips open.

In spite of herself she gave no resistance as he slowly and voluptuously explored her mouth; she couldn't. He only had to touch her—he'd only ever had to touch her—and she melted, turning liquid with desire. Her attraction to him had always been consuming, that was why she had tried to put distance between them after they'd lost Matthew. First by shutting herself away emotionally and mentally, and then by physically removing herself from his orbit. But he had forced his way into her life again, with disastrous results. But no, she couldn't think of their baby as a disaster.

With her guard lowered and her defences down, Melanie kissed him back as she had done on the fateful night in August. His sharp intake of breath told her he'd sensed her capitulation, but his mouth was like a drug and she couldn't break its hold on her.

It was another car drawing alongside them that caused Forde to ease back into his own seat, his mouth reluctantly leaving hers after one last long kiss at the side of her mouth.

To her shame, Melanie knew she wouldn't have been able to show such restraint, regardless of who was around. And that was the trouble, she told herself silently as she smoothed back a strand of hair off one hot cheek. Forde had been the chink in the armour she'd worn against the outside world from the day she had met him. He had made her believe in happy-ever-after for a while, convinced her that his love was enough to protect her from anything that might come against them, from within and without. But he hadn't been able to stop her hurting Matthew.

A young mother with a toddler climbed out of the car that had parked next to them, clearly pregnant for the second time. The girl didn't look a day over eighteen and she was bright-eyed and bushy-tailed, her long blonde hair and short miniskirt, which revealed endless legs clad in leggings, making Melanie feel like an old hag.

That was the sort of woman Forde should have married, she thought miserably. Someone fresh and sparkling without any hang-ups. Someone as far removed from herself as the man in the moon, in fact. Her thoughts gave strength to her voice when she said, 'I have to get back to work, Forde. Now.'

He didn't argue this time. 'OK. But you make sure you explain this new turn of events to James, Nell. I have a spy in the camp who'll inform me if you're not behaving, remember that.'

He had been joking, well, half joking, she surmised, but the words were like a bucket of cold water poured over her head. *Isabelle*. This baby was her *grandchild*. The panic returned but stronger, and she felt she must know what a fish felt like when caught in a fisherman's net with no visible source of escape.

'Eight o'clock tonight, OK?'

Forde was looking at her and, seeing in his eyes he wouldn't take no for an answer, Melanie nodded jerkily.

He gave her one last swift kiss, his uneven mouth quirking. 'Stop looking as though the prospect of dinner with the father of your child is a fate worse than death,' he murmured sardonically. 'My ego has taken enough hits in the last months as it is.'

Afterwards, she wondered what on earth had made her say her next words. Maybe it was because the memory of the woman's voice in the background when she'd been talking to him on the phone still rankled—more than rankled, if she was being honest. Or perhaps it was his assumption that the fact that she was pregnant sorted all the problems? Or that he didn't understand, he simply didn't *get* the torment she'd been going through since Matthew's death because she, and she alone, was responsible for their son's stillbirth and nothing could change that.

'I'm sure there are plenty of willing fingers just itching to stroke that ego though,' she said with deliberate nonchalance.

She watched the beautiful silver-blue eyes turn to crystal hardness. And immediately regretted her rashness.

'Now that was definitely loaded,' he said, searching her face with laserlike intensity. 'Explain.'

She shrugged. 'Nothing *to* explain. I was just saying I'm sure there are more than a few women lined up who are quite happy to keep you company, that's all.' Ecstatically so, no doubt.

'And on what do you base that assumption?' he asked with deceptive mildness.

'Forde, I'm fully aware I have no right to criticise

you seeing other women. You are free to do whatever you please.'

'Is that so?' It was a snarl. 'And this—' he held up his left hand with the thick gold wedding band '—means nothing? Is that it? Well, think again, sweetheart. It means a great deal to me as it happens.'

The hypocrisy was too much. 'I know someone was with you the night I phoned about the divorce papers,' she said stonily.

'What?' His brow wrinkled, then cleared. 'Yes, you're right,' he said with silky smoothness. 'There were several people present actually. I was holding a dinner party for my mother's birthday, just her and several old friends of hers. I don't know who you heard, Melanie, but I can assure you every woman present was eighty years old or above.'

Wonderful, just wonderful. Not only had she forgotten Isabelle's birthday but had revealed herself as a jealous, mean-minded shrew. Gathering the remnants of her dignity around her, she stared at him, her chin lifting. 'I see, but you don't have to explain to me. I was just saying you're free to do whatever you please.'

'No, Nell, I'm not.'

The return of his pet name for her after the Melanie of a few moments ago made her want to sag with relief. But she didn't. Stubbornly, she began, 'I have no right—'

'You have every right to demand of me the same faithfulness and honesty I demand of you, Nell. And let me just say this for the record. When I made my wedding vows I meant every one of them. And they hold firm. Got it?' Forde was secretly rather pleased at the

jealousy she'd betrayed but knew better than to bela-
bour the point. 'And I'll pick you up at eight tonight.'

She wanted to object but when she looked at him
there was an unsettling blend of concern and tenderness in his face. It wiped away her resolve. Weakly, she
said, 'James should never have said anything to your
mother. I'm not pleased with him.'

'Be as hard on him as you like,' Forde said cheerfully,
'but he *did* say something and I'll be at yours at eight.'
He opened the truck door and then paused, turning to
face her once more. 'You *were* going to tell me about
the baby, weren't you?'

His uncertainty made her feel like the worst sinner
on earth. She answered with obvious sincerity, her voice
soft. 'You would have been the first to know, Forde,
even if you hadn't turned up here this morning.' And
then honesty forced her to continue, 'But it might not
have been for a day or two until I'd adjusted to the idea.'

He stared at her. 'Is it really so bad, being pregnant
with our baby?'

It was the worst thing and the best thing in the world,
but how could she explain that to him when she couldn't
explain it to herself? 'I have to go,' she said tightly.

He nodded. 'Drive carefully.' And then, as an af-
terthought, he added, 'What are you going to tell my
mother? She's worried about you, Nell.'

She bit down hard on her bottom lip. 'The truth, I
guess.' But that was going to be nearly as painful as these
last few minutes with Forde. Isabelle wouldn't understand why, in these new circumstances, they weren't getting back together for a start, and who could blame her?

This was such a mess. *She* was a mess. And things

were going to get even messier in the next days when Forde realised she wasn't going back to him.

Her voice brittle, she said, 'Goodbye, Forde. And—and thank you for coming.'

He smiled. 'You don't have to thank me. I'm your husband, remember?'

He stood and watched her as she drove away, his hands thrust in his pockets and his shoulders slightly hunched. He looked big and solid and very sexy, and she was indisputably pregnant by this wonderful man who was also her husband. She should have been the happiest woman in the world…

CHAPTER SEVEN

ISABELLE must have been by the window looking out for her, because the minute she drove onto the drive and parked the truck, the front door opened. 'Melanie, dear.' Isabelle was leaning on the stick she'd used since the accident with her hip. 'Could you spare a moment or two before you go through to the garden?' she called as Melanie slammed the truck door.

Better to get it straight over with, Melanie told herself as she obediently followed Forde's mother into the house.

'I was just making a pot of coffee and was going to take a cup to dear James with a slice of the fruit cake he likes,' Isabelle said, leading the way into her farmhouse-style kitchen. James had become 'dear James' very quickly, which didn't surprise Melanie in the least. 'Sit yourself down while I see to him, and perhaps you'd like to cut yourself a slice of cake and pour us both a cup while I'm gone?'

Overcome with the strangest urge to burst into tears for the second time that morning, Melanie didn't trust herself to speak, merely nodding and smiling. In the days when she had still been with Forde she had spent many mornings helping Isabelle with something in the garden, and their eleven o'clock coffee and cake break had been something she'd looked forward to. A time of cosy chats and laughter. But she didn't think there'd be much laughter today.

Isabelle's fruit cake was one of her mother-in-law's specialities and, in spite of how she was feeling, Melanie discovered she was ravenously hungry, having skipped breakfast that morning after oversleeping. She'd done that more than once recently due to tossing and turning for the first part of the night and then falling into a deep sleep as dawn began to break. Consequently she felt tired all the time. Or she'd put down the exhaustion she felt lately to that, she thought, biting into a hefty piece of cake. Now, of course, she understood there was another factor too. In the early days with Matthew she'd felt drained.

Isabelle came back, beaming as she said, 'Such a nice boy, that James, but I don't think he eats enough living with those friends of his. He always wolfs down his cake as though he's starving.' The silver-blue eyes fastened on Melanie. 'And you, dear? Are you eating enough? You've looked a little peaky lately, if you don't mind me saying so, and James said you'd gone to the doctor's this morning?'

Melanie swallowed a mouthful of cake and nodded. 'I have been feeling unwell but there's nothing wrong, not exactly. I—I didn't realise but—' she took a deep breath; this was harder than she'd expected with Isabelle's sweet, concerned face in front of her '—I'm expecting a baby. Forde's baby,' she added hastily, just in case her mother-in-law got the wrong idea.

Isabelle's face was the third that morning to register stunned surprise, but she recovered herself almost immediately. 'Well, that's wonderful, dear,' she said warmly, reaching out and squeezing Melanie's hand. 'When is the baby due?'

'In the spring, May time.' It was so like Isabelle not to ask the obvious questions, Melanie thought gratefully, but feeling obligated to explain a little, she said, 'Forde came to see me one night in August to discuss— Well, to discuss my doing the work here actually. And—and one thing led to another...' She stopped helplessly.

'Well, I'm thrilled for you both,' Isabelle said briskly. 'Does Forde know?'

Melanie nodded. 'He came to the surgery as I was leaving.' Then quickly, before she lost her nerve, she said, 'This doesn't mean we—we're getting back together, Isabelle.'

There was a moment's silence. Then Isabelle said gently, 'Do I take it you don't love him any more?'

'*No*. I mean, I do love Forde. Of course I do.'

'And I know he loves you. Deeply. So forgive me but I don't quite understand...'

Melanie tried, she really tried to keep back the tears but it was hopeless. And this wasn't polite, ladylike weeping either. She wailed heartbrokenly, her eyes gushing and her nose running, and even when she felt Isabelle's arms go round her with a strength that belied their frailty, she couldn't pull herself together. She was crying for Matthew, for her dear little boy, and for Forde, for the way she had broken his heart when they'd lost their son, for all the smashed dreams and hopes that had turned to ashes. And for this new baby, this tiny, little person who hadn't asked to exist and who was so vulnerable...

When her cries had dwindled to hiccuping sobs, Isabelle fetched a cold flannel and towel and mopped her face as though she were three years old instead of nearly thirty. Utterly spent, Melanie sat quiet and docile, her head aching and her eyes burning as her mother-in-law made a fresh pot of coffee. Once they both had a steaming mug in front of them, Isabelle sat down at the kitchen table with her and took Melanie's hands in her own parchment-like ones. 'Talk to me,' she said softly.

Melanie shook her head slowly. 'Oh, Isabelle, I don't know how to explain.'

The old lady sighed. 'You're the daughter I never had, you know that, don't you? And that will never change, whatever the future holds. But this blaming yourself for something that wasn't your fault has to stop, child.'

Melanie looked at her through tear-drenched eyes. 'I don't feel I have the right to be happy again, not after losing Matthew, and I'm frightened...'

'What?' Isabelle pressed, when Melanie paused.

'I'm frightened something will happen to Forde if I'm with him, and now this baby too.' Instinctively she put a protective hand on her stomach. 'I think I'm perhaps meant to be alone, Isabelle.'

'Nonsense, dear.' Isabelle never minced words. 'You had a terrible and tragic accident, and on top of that woman's curse of hormones came into play, colouring your thinking and causing the depression you're still suffering from. If you had taken the medication the doctor prescribed you might be feeling better by now.'

Melanie's chin came up. 'I didn't want to. Matthew

deserved to have me grieve for him. It was all I *could* do.' She retrieved her hands, wiping her eyes and blowing her nose before she said, 'I know you mean well, Isabelle, but I have to work out what I'm going to do in my own way.'

'Yes, dear, I know that, but will you do one thing for me? For all of us? See Forde now and again. He loves you very much. Just talk to him, explain how you feel, even if it doesn't make sense. Don't shut him out, not now. This is his child too.'

Melanie nodded. 'I know that,' she said, through the tightness in her throat. 'And—and I'm seeing him tonight.'

'Good.' Isabelle's voice became brisk. 'Now, drink your coffee and have another piece of cake. Two, if you wish. You have to keep your strength up and you're eating for two, remember.'

Making a great effort, Melanie responded to the lightening of the conversation. 'The health experts would take you to task for that thinking these days.'

'No doubt, but I've never yet listened to what the experts say, and I'm not about to start now.' Isabelle chuckled. 'I'm an irksome old lady, I know.'

Melanie smiled, her voice soft. 'You're a lovely old lady,' she said, with a tenderness that brought moisture to Isabelle's eyes.

Melanie had two more pieces of cake and they talked about the progress of the garden and the weather and other such non-intrusive subjects before she left the house and went outside to break the news to James, whereupon Isabelle immediately picked up the telephone and called Forde.

James was busy working on the large informal pond Isabelle had requested in a low-lying area of the garden, his artfully random arrangement of large stones enhancing the soft outlines and sinuous curves of the water feature. Knowing how passionate Isabelle was about wildlife, Melanie had suggested the margins of the pool be masked by soft, naturalistic planting, which extended into the shallows to provide safe shelter for fish fry, amphibians, and bathing or drinking birds.

He looked up as she approached, his gaze taking in her red-rimmed eyes and pink nose, and his face was openly apprehensive as he stood up.

'I'm fine, don't worry,' Melanie said before he could speak. 'But there's something I've got to tell you because I won't be lifting or carrying anything heavy for a while. I'm having a baby.'

James took a step backwards as though she was going to deliver on the spot. 'What?' he all but screeched.

Melanie laughed; she couldn't help it.

Smiling sheepishly, James said, 'Forde?'

She nodded. 'Of course. Who else?'

'So you're back together?'

'Not exactly.' But a reasonable assumption, she supposed.

'Right.'

Not for the first time Melanie blessed the fact that James was the sort of easy-going soul who accepted people for exactly what they were. She was going to have enough explaining to do to various folk over the next months, but with James no explanation was necessary. 'The baby will be born early May, which isn't the best time, I know. We usually get busy then after the winter.'

'No sweat.' James grinned at her. 'We'll manage.'

'I've been thinking for a while of getting someone else on board, perhaps over the next weeks would be a good idea so we're ready for the spring?' And then, in case he thought he was being usurped, she added, 'They could be your assistant.'

He nodded. 'Whatever you think.'

She smiled, and they began to get on with some work, but Melanie's mind was buzzing. James had said 'whatever you think,' but that was the thing—she didn't know what she thought about anything any more. Except that she loved this baby with every fibre of her being. She hadn't known of its existence this time yesterday, but now it was the centre of her universe.

For the rest of the day she worked automatically, her mind a seething cauldron of hope and doubts and fears, but as she drove home from Isabelle's in a deep November twilight she felt she knew what she had to do. Maybe she had known it from the moment Dr Chisholm had told her she was carrying Forde's child. She just hadn't been able to bear acknowledging it.

It was dark by the time she parked the truck and walked wearily into the cottage. Once inside, she went through the routine of a working day—outdoor clothes and boots left in the kitchen, upstairs to strip off and then a hot bath. It was close to seven o'clock when she emerged from the bathroom, pink and warm after a long soak, and once in the bedroom she knew she just had to lie down for a few minutes before she began to get ready to go out with Forde. She was so tired she felt drugged.

Promising herself she would simply shut her eyes for a little while and relax her aching muscles, she snuggled under the duvet, and was asleep as her head touched the pillow.

CHAPTER EIGHT

FORDE knew he had a fight on his hands. He would have known that without his mother's phone call earlier in the day, but when she'd repeated her conversation with Melanie it had confirmed everything Janet had spoken about.

He frowned to himself as he drove the miles to Melanie's cottage. Damn it, he didn't understand her. He loved her, more than life itself, but this consuming need to punish herself—and indirectly him—for something that neither of them had been able to prevent was something outside his comprehension. And this idea of hers that she brought misfortune on those she cared about was sheer garbage. His mother was convinced the idea had taken root even before they'd married due to Melanie's past, and the miscarriage had given credence to something that would have faded away in time, shrivelled into nothing when it hadn't been given sustenance. But the accident had happened.

He gripped the steering wheel, his face grim. And the seed of this nonsense had been watered and fed by her depression that had followed.

He realised he was so tense his body was as tight as piano wire and forced himself to consciously relax, expelling a deep breath as he stepped on the brake. He'd been driving far too fast, way over the speed limit.

What the hell was he going to do? How could he convince her that life without her was an empty void, devoid of any real joy or satisfaction? In her crazy, mixed-up mind she thought she was protecting him in some way by cutting the threads that bound them. In reality she was killing him, inch by inch. And now there was the baby, a product of their love. Because it *had* been love that had given it life; this child had been created by passion and desire certainly—he only had to look at her to become rock hard—but love had been the foundation of their relationship from their first date. *Before* their first date. He had been born waiting for Melanie to appear in his life and he had recognised she was his other half early on. It really had been as simple as that.

A fox skittered across the road a little way ahead of him, a flash of red and bushy tail in the headlights. It was a timely reminder he was still going too fast and he checked his speed accordingly. He'd driven the car too hard too often lately—yet another indication that his normal self-control wasn't as sharp as it could be. The trouble was, thoughts of Melanie were always at the forefront of his mind, thoughts that triggered a whole gamut of emotion and tied him up in knots. His mother had told him she was worried Melanie would crack up completely if something didn't give soon and it had been on the tip of his tongue to say her son was in the same boat.

He smiled grimly to himself. He hadn't, of course. His mother was concerned enough as it was. And it would have been a trite remark anyway. He had no intention of going to pieces. He was going to get his wife back come hell or high water, and the news about the baby only meant it would be sooner rather than later. He was done with the softly-softly approach and pretending to play along with the divorce. When she had first left him he'd told her she would divorce him over his dead body and that still held.

Forde glanced at the huge bunch of pink rosebuds and baby's breath on the passenger seat at the side of him, next to the bottle of sparkling wine—non-alcoholic of course. Melanie had been obsessional regarding eating and drinking all the right things when she'd been pregnant before.

His brooding gaze softened. She'd pored over all the baby books she had bought, drunk gallons of milk, and the first time she had felt flutterings in her belly that were definitely tiny limbs thrashing about had been beside herself with joy. She would make a wonderful mother; he knew that. Her experiences as a child had made her determined their child would know nothing but love and security. He would remind her of that tonight if she persisted in this ridiculous notion of continuing with the separation.

He began to mentally list all the arguments and counter arguments he would put to Melanie to support his cause for the rest of the journey, playing devil's advocate some of the time until he was absolutely sure she couldn't put anything to him he hadn't thought about.

When he parked in the little car park belonging to the row of cottages he was feeling positive. She loved him and he loved her, that was the most important thing to remember, that and the miracle that their night of love in the summer had made a little person, a composite of them both. She couldn't dispute that. Come the spring there was going to be clear evidence of it. A baby boy or girl, a living, breathing reality.

He felt such a surge of love for Melanie and his unborn child that it took his breath away. He'd been wrong when he'd thought she partly blamed him for Matthew's death; he realised that now after talking to Janet and his mother. Melanie had condemned herself utterly. Maybe he should have refused to let her withdraw from him in those early days after the miscarriage? The doctors had told him to give her time, that it was natural for some women to detach themselves from what had happened for a while, nature's way of assisting the mind to deal with something too devastating to take in all in one go.

But it hadn't been like that with Melanie. Why had he listened to anyone when all his instincts had been telling him to *make* her let him in? He hadn't known if he was on foot or horseback, that was the trouble. They had still been wrapped up in the rosy glow of finding each other and getting married, then the thrill of finding out she was pregnant—life had been perfect, scarily so with hindsight. And then, in the space of a heartbeat, their world had fragmented. He could still remember her face when he'd got to the hospital and found her in labour...

He shook his head to dispel the image that had haunted him ever since.

Getting out of the car, he looked towards the cottages. If he had his way she would be returning home with him tonight. Janet had told him not to take no for an answer when he'd told her everything earlier that day, which was all very well, but this *was* Melanie they were talking about. A corner of his mouth twisted wryly. She might look as though a puff of wind could blow her away, but his wife was one tough cookie when she had the bit between her teeth about something or other.

An owl hooted somewhere close by, otherwise the night was still and quiet, unlike his churning mind. He took a deep breath and composed himself, feeling like a soldier preparing himself for battle. Which wasn't too far from the truth, he thought sardonically. And Melanie was one hell of a formidable opponent...

At Melanie's front door, he took another deep breath but didn't pause as he rang the doorbell. He had expected some lights to be on downstairs but the place seemed to be in darkness. He frowned, waiting a few moments before ringing again. Nothing. He glanced at his watch. A couple of minutes to eight. Surely she wouldn't have gone out to avoid him? But no, Melanie wouldn't do that, he told himself in the next moment, ashamed the thought had come into his mind. Whatever else, Melanie wasn't a coward, neither did she break her word. She had said she would be here so what was wrong?

Concerned now, he threw caution to the wind and banged on the door consistently with all his might. The cottages either side of Melanie were in blackness, but there was a light on in one a couple of doors down. He'd go there in a minute if he had to. Her truck had been in the car park—he'd parked right next to it—so she couldn't have gone far. Unless she was lying injured inside...

He knew a moment of gut-wrenching relief when the door creaked open. Melanie stood there in the robe she'd worn that night in August, her eyes heavy-lidded with sleep and her blonde hair tousled. 'Forde?' Her voice was husky, slow. 'What time is it? I only meant to have a rest for a few minutes.'

'Eight o'clock.' He had a job to speak. From being worried to death about her, he now found himself wanting to ravish her to heaven and back in her deliciously dishevelled state.

He gave her the flowers before bending to pick up the bottle he'd put down in order to batter the door, his body so hard with desire it was painful to walk when she said, 'Come in, and thank you for the flowers. Rosebuds and baby's breath, my favourite.'

'I know.' He smiled and received a small smile in return as she turned away. He followed her into the house. Unlike the previous time he was here she didn't suggest he sit in the sitting room like a guest, but led the way to the kitchen.

'I'm sorry, I'm not ready,' she said flusteredly, stating the obvious as she rummaged about for a vase in one of the cupboards. 'It'll take me a few minutes. Can I get you something to drink while you wait? Coffee, juice, a glass of wine?'

'A coffee would be great.' He didn't really want one; he just didn't want her to fly off upstairs immediately. On impulse, he said, 'We don't have to go out for a meal tonight if you're tired. I can order something in. Chinese, Indian, Thai? Whatever you fancy.'

He could see her mind working as she looked at him. Going out for a meal would be less intimate, less cosy, but the thought of not having to dress up and make the effort to go out was clearly tempting. He waited without saying anything. She fiddled with the flowers as the rich smell of coffee began to fill the room, but he still didn't speak.

'There's a Chinese in the next village,' she volunteered after a few moments. 'The leaflet's under the biscuit tin there.' She pointed to a tin close to where he'd sat himself on one of the two kitchen stools tucked under the tiny breakfast bar. 'Perhaps you could order while I get dressed.'

'You don't have to on my account.'

Her whole demeanour changed and he could have kicked himself. 'Joke,' he said lightly, although it hadn't altogether been. 'What would you like?'

'Anything, I don't mind.' She clearly couldn't wait to escape. 'Help yourself to coffee. I won't be long,' she added as she turned away.

He sat for a moment after she had gone and then stirred himself to pour a mug of coffee. Melanie looked exhausted and no wonder—she'd been living on her nerves for well over twelve months now. She was like a cat on a hot tin roof most of the time. A soft, warm, blonde cat with big wary eyes and the sweetest face, but a cat that was nonetheless quite liable to show its claws if the occasion warranted it.

Forde reached for the menu under the biscuit tin and glanced through it. He was absolutely starving, he decided, and quite able to do justice to double helpings. After a little deliberation he thought one of the set dinners would be a good idea to give Melanie plenty of choice. He picked up the telephone and ordered one that was allegedly for three people comprising of sweet and sour chicken Cantonese style; king prawn, mushrooms and green peppers in spicy black bean sauce; shrimp egg Foo Young, chicken in orange sauce; beef with ginger and spring onion; dry special fried rice and prawn crackers.

Walking through to the dining room, he found the table was relatively clear, just a file or two piled in one corner. Placing these on the floor, he dug and delved until he found cutlery, place mats, napkins and glasses. Then he returned to the kitchen and poured himself another coffee.

Ridiculously he found he was nervous, his stomach full of butterflies as it had been on their first date. It had been the evening after they had met at their mutual friend's wedding; he hadn't been able to wait for more than twenty-four hours to see her again. He had wined and dined her in a plush restaurant, playing up to the image of wealthy, successful tycoon while being inwardly terrified the whole time she wouldn't want to see him again. She had invited him in for a coffee when he had dropped her back to her bedsit—just a coffee, she'd emphasised.

They had talked for three hours.

He smiled to himself, remembering how it had been. He had never talked to a woman like that before in the whole of his life but with Melanie it had seemed right, natural to keep nothing back. And she had been the same. Or he'd thought she had.

Restlessly, he walked over to the back door and opened it, stepping into the tiny garden. The night was chilly but not overly cold, and from the light of the house he saw the small space had been trimmed and manicured for the winter. The heady scent of the roses was gone but a softer perfume was in the air and he saw several shrubs in large pots were flowering.

He wasn't aware of Melanie behind him until she said, 'I still like splashes of colour in the winter. That's a Viburnum bodnantense in the corner. Pretty, isn't it, with those clusters of dark pink flowers? And the Oregon grape is about as robust as you can get and I love the way its foliage turns red in winter. I've planted several in Isabelle's garden.'

He glanced down at her as she moved to stand with him. She had dressed in a soft white woolly jumper and jeans, and her pale blonde hair was pulled into a shining ponytail. She wore no make-up and she looked about sixteen, he thought shakily, swamped with a love so fierce it took a moment before he could say, 'Is that where the scent is coming from?'

'Oh, you mean the winter honeysuckle.' She pointed to a shrub close to the wall of the house. 'It's called Winter Beauty and it flowers right through the winter into the spring. Beautiful, isn't it?'

'Yes,' he said, not taking his eyes from her face. 'Very beautiful.'

She looked up at him and he saw a tremor go through her. 'You're cold.' He took her arm and turned her into the warmth of the house. She felt fragile under his fingers, as though if he pressed too hard she'd break. Warning himself to go carefully, he kept his voice light when he said, 'There's plenty of coffee left. Shall I pour you a cup?'

She shook her head. 'I'd love one but I'm limited to one or two cups of tea or coffee a day now. Caffeine, you know.'

It brought back memories of what had seemed like an endless list of dos and don'ts when she'd been pregnant before, and not for the first time he reflected that there were women who ate and drank what they liked, smoked, even took drugs, and went on to have healthy babies, whereas Melanie… Not that he agreed with such a selfish approach, of course, but Melanie had done everything right first time round. It seemed the height of unfairness she'd lost Matthew the way she had. Quietly, Forde said, 'Juice, then? Or shall we open that bottle of fizzy grape juice I brought? Non-alcoholic, by the way.'

She had walked into the kitchen so that the breakfast bar was between them, and everything about her suggested she wasn't about to lower her guard in any way. Her body language was confirmed when she said, 'Forde, I agreed to see you tonight but I don't want you to think it means anything other than I recognise we must talk. This baby is as much yours as mine. I know that.'

It was something. Not much, but better than having to persuade her to face that very fact.

'The thing is,' she began hesitantly, only to pause when he lifted his hand palm up.

'We're not talking about "the thing" or anything else until we've eaten.' He was going to have to fight to get through to her and he was quite prepared for that, but he was damned if he was going to do it on an empty stomach. 'The food should be here any minute, OK?'

As though on cue the doorbell rang.

Within a minute or two the table was groaning under an array of fragrant, steaming foil dishes and a positive banquet was spread out in front of them.

Far from picking at her food, as Forde had feared, Melanie ate like a hungry cat, delicately but with an intensity that meant she more than did justice to the meal. There were only a few morsels left by the time they were both replete, and as Melanie leant back in her chair she sighed blissfully. 'That was delicious. I didn't realise I was so hungry.'

He grinned. 'Eating for two, sweetheart.'

A shadow passed over her face. 'Forde—'

'Or maybe three. It could be twins. There are twins on my father's side, remember, so who knows?'

Her eyes wide with something like alarm in them, Melanie said weakly, 'I'm going for a scan this week. I'll let you know if there's two.'

'Twins would be great,' he said, tongue in cheek. 'Double the joy.'

'And double the feeding, changing nappies—' She stopped suddenly, as though she had been reminded of something. 'Forde, we have to talk. Now.'

'OK.' He smiled as though his heart hadn't gone into spasm at the look on her face. Whatever she was going to say, he knew he wouldn't like it. 'Let's go into the sitting room with our drinks, shall we?'

She had relaxed when they were eating, even allowing herself to laugh a few times at the stories he'd purposely told against himself, but now she was as stiff as a board as he followed her into the other room. She chose to curl up on one of the sofas in a way that meant he was forced to take the other one.

'So?' He found he was done with prevaricating. 'What do you want to say, Nell?'

He watched her take a deep breath and it caused him to tense still more.

'I—I can't keep this baby when it's born. If—if you want to I think you should take it.'

Whatever he'd prepared himself for, it wasn't this. He knew his mouth had fallen open, and shut it with a little snap, trying desperately to hang onto reality. 'What did you say?'

'It would be better if it was brought up by one of its natural parents,' Melanie said woodenly. 'And you have your mother and a whole host of relations. It—it would have roots, a sense of belonging, and you're wealthy enough to hire the best nanny, and there's Janet too—'

'What are you talking about?' Only the sure knowledge this wasn't really what she wanted enabled Forde to keep his temper. 'The best nanny in the world is no compensation for a child's mother, a mother who would love it beyond imagination in your case. You were born to be a mother, Nell. You know that as well as I do.'

'No,' she said in a stony voice. 'I can't keep it.'

Struggling for calmness, he said, 'Why not? Explain. You owe me that, not to mention our unborn child. Have you considered how our son or daughter is going to feel when it finds out its mother wanted nothing to do with it after it was born?'

She shut her eyes for an infinitesimal moment. 'That's not fair.'

'The hell it isn't. Face facts, woman.'

'*I am facing facts.*'

The loss of control was so sudden he jumped visibly as she sprang to her feet.

'If I keep it, if I'm its mother, something will happen. Like it did with Matthew. Or to you. Something will happen to stop us being a family and it will be because of me. Don't you understand that yet? It's because I love it I have to stay out of its life.'

He stared at her. She was standing with her hands clenched into fists at her sides, her body as straight as a board, and he could see she believed every word. Softly, he said, 'And that's why you walked out on me, on our marriage.' It was a statement, not a question. But he had to make her hear herself, acknowledge the enormity of what she had confessed. 'Because you've told yourself this lie so often you believe it.'

It was dawning on him just how much he had failed her. He should have insisted she went for counselling after Matthew's death, forced her to confront the gremlins, but he had been so frightened of causing her more pain. Of losing her. Ironic.

'It's not a lie.' She drew in a shuddering breath.

'Oh, yes, it is.' He stood up and crossed the space between them, taking her stiff, unyielding body into his arms. 'Life doesn't come in neat, sanitised packages, Nell. People die in accidents, of diseases, of old age, in—in miscarriages and stillbirths and a whole host of other medical issues. It isn't nice and it isn't fair but it happens. You weren't to blame for Matthew's death. I don't know why it happened and I have to confess I've shouted and railed at God ever since because of it, but I *do* know you weren't to blame. You've got to get that into your head.'

'I can't.' She pulled away, stepping back from him. 'And I've got to protect this baby, Forde. If you take it and I stay out of your lives it will be all right.'

Her white face and haunted eyes warned Forde that he had pushed her to the limit of her endurance. His mind now working rapidly, he kept his voice steady and low. 'It goes without saying I'll take our baby, Nell. But I think you owe it one thing. I want you to go and talk over how you feel with someone who is completely unbiased and who has experience in the type of grief you're feeling. Will you do that for it? And me?'

She'd taken another step backwards. 'A doctor, you mean? You think I'm crazy?'

'Not in a million years.' He wouldn't let her retreat further, covering the distance between them in one stride and taking her cold hands in his. 'But I know someone, a friend, who's trained in this type of counselling. She offered to talk to you months ago in a professional role, just you and her and everything confidential between the two of you, OK? You'd like Miriam, Nell. I promise.'

She extracted her hands from his. 'I don't know.'

'Then trust me to know. Will you do that? And what have you got to lose? I love you, Nell. I'll always love you. If you won't do this for yourself, do it for me.'

He saw the confusion in her eyes and, acting on instinct, he reached out and touched her cheek. Her skin was soft like raw silk and as warm as liquid honey. Leaning closer, he bent his head and kissed her, a gentle, undemanding kiss, before drawing her against him.

They stood together in the quiet room, Forde nuzzling the top of her head and Melanie resting against his chest without speaking. Her hair smelt of the apple shampoo she favoured and there was the faintest scent of vanilla from her perfume. Why two such fairly innocuous fragrances should make his blood pulse with desire he didn't know, but then Melanie had always had that effect on him. He wanted her so badly he ached with it, but he steeled himself against betraying it, knowing at this moment she wanted nothing more than to be held and comforted.

After a minute or two, he murmured, 'I'll ring Miriam tomorrow and ask her to see you. She's a busy lady but we go way back and I know she'll find time.'

Melanie was quiet for a moment, then her voice came faintly muffled from his chest. 'Way back? What does that mean?'

He caught the tinge of jealousy she was trying to conceal and almost smiled. 'She's the mother of a close friend, grandmother of six and has been happily married for forty years.' Miriam was also much sought after and at the top of her field professionally, but he wasn't about to mention that.

'Forde, it won't change anything. You know that, don't you?' She raised swimming eyes to his. 'You have to face the inevitable. I have.'

'Go and see her, that's all I'm asking,' he said softly. He kissed her again, and in spite of telling himself to go carefully it deepened into something more than comfort. A restless urgency surfaced and he knew she felt it too by the way she clung to him in a hungry response that took the last of his control. His hands roamed over her body, touching her with sensual, intimate caresses, and then he scooped her up in his arms as he murmured against her lips, 'I want you. Tonight. But if you want me to leave now, I'll go.'

Her answer was to kiss him with a desire that was

unmistakable, and with a small growl Forde carried her up the stairs to the bedroom. He laid her on the bed and in frantic haste and without speaking they tore off their clothes and then he lay down beside her, cupping her face in his palms and kissing her deeply and passionately.

She had always been a lover who gave as much as she got and now her hands and mouth explored him as hungrily as his did her, twisting and turning with him as they moaned their pleasure. Her breasts felt fuller in his hands and as he took one rosy nipple in his mouth she arched with a little cry.

'They—they're more sensitive now,' she gasped against what he was doing to her, and as his mouth returned to hers he swept his tongue inside and then pulled back and bit her bottom lip gently.

'You're so beautiful, my love,' he murmured shakily. 'I don't think I can wait much longer.'

'Then don't.'

She was wet and warm for him when he entered her. She hooked her legs round him and raised her hips and they moved together in perfect unison towards a release that had them both calling out as they tipped over the edge into white pleasure. Then he circled her in his arms, one thigh lying over hers as she opened drugged eyes. 'You don't know how many cold showers I've taken in the middle of the night recently,' he murmured wryly.

She half smiled, but he could see she was thinking again. 'Forde, we shouldn't have—'

'Yes, we should.' He brushed back a strand of hair

from her face. 'I wanted you and you wanted me. It was that simple. Don't try to complicate it.'

'But it doesn't—'

'Change anything,' he finished for her. 'Yes, I know. Don't worry. Go to sleep.' He pulled the duvet over them.

Her expression was one of total confusion and remorse. 'It's not fair to you,' she whispered.

'Nell, believe me, I can live with this sort of unfairness,' he said drily.

She smiled again but a proper smile this time and he grinned back at her. 'Go to sleep,' he said again, kissing the tip of her nose and then her mouth. 'Everything's OK.'

She was asleep within moments, snuggled close to him, but Forde lay and watched her for a long, long time. *Everything's OK.* What a stupid thing to say, he thought ruefully. His wife had told him she was going to hand over their baby to him at birth and then disappear out of their lives, and he'd said everything was OK. But he had no intention of letting her do that, not for a second, so maybe everything was, if not OK, then clearer than it had been for a good while.

With a feather-light touch he reached out his fingers and ran them across her belly. It might be his imagination but already he thought he could feel a slight swell. His child was alive in there, tiny now but each day gaining strength.

Tears pricked at the backs of his eyes. It had been a long, hard road since they'd lost Matthew, and they still weren't at the end of it yet, not by a long chalk, but against all the odds a miracle had happened and

Melanie was pregnant. That one night of loving had produced this baby and no matter what he had to do to achieve it, they were going to be a family. If he had to kidnap Melanie and take her and their baby to some remote place in the back of beyond until she accepted that, he'd do it.

She stirred in her sleep, murmuring his name before breathing steadily and quietly once more.

It was a tiny thing, but it cheered him. She was his. End of story, he thought fiercely. And promptly fell asleep.

CHAPTER NINE

MELANIE woke first the next morning, aware she was wonderfully warm and cosy and sleepy. Then her eyes snapped open. *Forde.* He was curled into her back, one male arm resting possessively across her stomach.

Very, very carefully she eased his arm off her and then turned to face him. He was fast asleep, the duvet down to his waist revealing his wide, muscled shoulders and the black curly body hair covering his chest. She drank him in for some moments and then slid silently out of bed. She didn't intend to sneak away like the time before, she wouldn't do that to him again, but neither did she want to pretend they were like any other couple waking up together.

Gathering her clothes in her arms, she padded through to the bathroom, locking the door behind her. When she emerged, fully clothed and coiffured, she glanced through the open bedroom door. Forde was sitting up in bed, his hands behind his head, and her heart raced like a runaway horse. He looked like every woman's fantasy of what she'd like to find in her Christmas stocking.

'Hi, sweetheart,' he said lazily. 'All finished in there?'

She nodded jerkily. And then found she couldn't tear

her eyes away as he flung back the duvet and stood up. She had seen him naked many times but she didn't think she would ever grow tired of looking at him. The flagrant maleness was intoxicating and he moved as beautifully as one of the big cats, his muscles sleek and honed and not an ounce of fat on his hard frame. He had almost reached her before she pulled herself together, but as she went to disappear down the stairs he turned her round with his hand on her arm. His kiss was firm and sweet but he didn't prolong the embrace, although as he turned away and strolled into the bathroom Melanie noticed a certain part of his anatomy was betraying his desire for her in the age-old way.

Heat slammed into her cheeks as she scurried downstairs, but then the faint feeling of sickness that would gather steam throughout the day before dispersing round seven or eight o'clock in the evening made itself felt. It was the one thing about pregnancy she truly hated, she told herself, forcing down a couple of dry biscuits once she reached the kitchen. Before she had become pregnant with Matthew she had always imagined morning sickness was just that—you woke up, you vomited, and then you got on with the rest of the day as right as rain. Instead this horrible nausea and the overall feeling of being unwell dogged her all day, but if this baby followed the same pattern as Matthew it would only be another two or three weeks before she felt better.

Melanie plugged in the coffee machine and then stood with her hands on her stomach, the wonder that a little life was growing inside her engulfing all her worries and fears and doubts for a few moments. 'You'll be told about your brother, little one, as soon as you're old enough to understand,' she whispered. 'He was our first child and greatly loved, but that doesn't mean you won't be loved too, for who and what you are.'

Would this baby understand that she had to leave it for its own good, though? Could any child take that on board? It might hate her. But would that matter so much if it was safe and protected and having a good life? The turmoil came in again on a great flood of anguish. She *was* doing the right thing, wasn't she? Yes, yes, she was. She couldn't doubt herself. And there must be no more nights like last night. This separation had to stand. And that meant she mustn't see Forde any more, because if he was there, in front of her, then all her resolve went out of the window. She wasn't strong enough where he was concerned.

'What's wrong?' said Forde sharply from behind her.

Melanie swung round, her hands springing away from her belly. 'Nothing, nothing's wrong.'

'You were standing there like that and for a minute I thought you were in pain,' he said thickly, his eyes searching her face as though he still wasn't quite sure if she was telling him the truth.

'I'm fine.' She took a deep breath. She had never voluntarily mentioned Matthew or what had happened, Forde had always been the one to broach the subject and more often than not then she had refused to discuss it, knowing she would break down if she did, but now she said quietly, 'I was thinking of Matthew, that's all. I—I don't want him forgotten. I want this baby to know it had a brother.'

'Of course.' His voice was soft but with a note in it that made her want to cry. 'That's taken as read, Nell.'

'Forde, if I agree to go and see Miriam, to talk to her, I want—' she took a deep breath '—I want you to promise you won't come here again. That's the deal. I mean it.'

She saw him take a physical step backwards as though she had slapped him across the face.

'We can't keep—' She shook her head. There was no kind way to say it. 'I don't want you here. It complicates everything and it will just make the final parting all the harder. I can cope on my own.'

'And if I can't? Cope, that is?' he said grimly. 'What then? Or is this all about you to the exclusion of anything else?'

Now she felt as though *he* had slapped *her*.

'You're carrying my child,' he said with deliberate control. 'That gives me certain rights, surely? You can't shut me out as though I don't exist.'

'I'm not trying to shut you out, not from the baby.'

'Oh, I see.' He raised dark brows. 'So I promise to stay away for the next nine months—'

'Six. I'm already three months pregnant.'

'Six months,' he continued as though she hadn't interrupted, 'and then what? I get a phone call saying the baby's born and I can come and pick it up? Is that what you've got planned?'

She stared at him. He had a right to be angry but now she was angry too. 'I didn't *have* to tell you I was pregnant,' she said stiffly. 'Not so early on anyway.'

'As I recall, it was me turning up at the doctor's that forced you to reveal it. Right? Whether you would have told me if you'd had time to think about it, I'm not so sure.'

Probably because he had touched on something she had been questioning herself about for the last twenty-four hours, Melanie was incensed. 'I'm not discussing this further, but I'd like you to remember that this is *my* house and I have a perfect right to say who comes over the threshold.' She glared at him, hands on hips and her eyes flashing.

'If you weren't pregnant I'd try shaking some sense into you,' he ground out between clenched teeth.

She knew he didn't mean it. Forde would never touch a woman in anger. Nevertheless her small chin rose a notch. 'You could try,' she said bitingly, 'but don't forget what I do for a living. I'm stronger than I look.'

'Actually, I've never doubted how strong you are,' he said tersely. 'It's your best and your worst attribute. It got you through the first twenty-five years of your life until you met me but now it's in danger of ruining the rest of your life. You need to let me in, Nell. You don't have to fight alone. Don't you realise that's what marriage is all about? I'm in your corner, for better or worse, richer or poorer, in sickness and health. I love you. *You.* The kind of love that will last for ever. I'm not going to give up on you whatever you say or do so get that through your head.'

'And you get through your head that I can't be what you want me to be. I'm not good for you, Forde. I'm not good for anyone.'

'You are the best thing that ever happened to me,' he said from the heart. 'The very best. Now you can try to tell yourself different if you like, but I know what I feel.'

She stared at him. 'I can't do this,' she said flatly, the

tone carrying more weight than any show of emotion.
'I want you to go, Forde. Now. I mean it.'

She did. He could see it in every fibre of her being.
But he had one last thing to say. 'Even before the accident, you were expecting the bubble to burst, Nell. It
became a self-fulfilling prophecy and you are the only
one who can change that. I don't think I can do or say
any more but I hope you have the courage to dig deep
and face what you need to face, for the sake of our child
as much as us.'

Her chin was up and her voice was tight and thin
when she said, 'Have you finished?'

He gave her one last long look and then walked into
the dining room, where his jacket was still hanging
over the back of a chair, shrugging it on and leaving
the house without another word.

Melanie heard the front door slam behind him but
she didn't move for a full minute simply because she
couldn't. She felt sick and ill and wretchedly unhappy,
but she told herself she'd done what had to be done.

After a while she poured herself a coffee because if
ever she had needed one it was now, walking into the
sitting room and sinking down on one of the sofas. She
sat for some time. It had started to rain outside, big
drops splattering against the window, and she shivered.
The weather was changing at last. Winter was round
the corner.

It was the following evening when her phone rang just
as she was finishing dinner. She hadn't felt like a meal,
but had forced herself to cook a cheese omelette after
she'd had her bath and changed into her pyjamas, con-

scious that she had to eat healthily now. To that end she'd had a glass of milk with the omelette and finished with an apple crumble and custard. Shop-bought but tasty nonetheless.

Her heart thudded as she picked up the phone but it wasn't Forde. Instead a woman's voice said, 'Can I speak to Mrs Masterson, please?'

'Speaking.' This had to be the woman Forde had mentioned.

'This is Miriam Cotton. Forde asked me to give you a ring.'

'Oh, yes.' Melanie suddenly felt ridiculously nervous. She didn't want to go and see a stranger and talk about her innermost feelings, but she had made a bargain with Forde that he'd leave her alone if she did so. 'I—I need to make an appointment, Mrs Cotton. I'm sure you're very busy so I quite understand it might not be for a while.'

It was another minute or two before she put down the phone and her head was spinning. She was going to see Miriam Cotton after work the next day. She didn't doubt that Forde had pulled strings to make it happen; 'strike while the iron was hot' was his style.

She sat and brooded for a good hour, looking at the address and telephone number Miriam had given her and wondering whether to call her back and cancel the appointment. It would mean she would have to take a change of clothes to work and get ready before she left Forde's mother's house, but that wasn't really the issue.

She was frightened. Scared stiff.

As the thought hit she realised her hands were clenched into fists in her lap and she concentrated on relaxing her fingers slowly. Forde had said she would have to find the courage to dig deep. Why should she put herself through that? What if it did no good? What if it made her feel even worse?

Panic rose, hot and strong, and then she remembered something else Forde had said, something she'd tried to put out of her mind, but which had only been relegated to the subconscious, waiting to jump out the minute she let it. He'd said she'd been expecting the bubble of their marriage to burst all along, that it had become a self-fulfilling prophecy and she was the only one who could change that. It had made her so mad she could have cheerfully strangled him, and she'd told herself at the time that was because it was untrue and terribly unfair.

She shut her eyes tightly. But it wasn't.

Opening her eyes, she stood up. She was exhausted; she couldn't think of this any more. She was going to bed and in the morning she would decide what she was going to do. But even as she thought it she knew her decision had already been made. Because something else Forde had said had cut deep. She had to do this for the sake of the baby. She had to *try*. It might be a lot of pain and anguish for nothing, and in digging up the past she might open a can of worms that was best left closed, but if she didn't try she would never know, would she?

She didn't even bother to brush her teeth before getting into bed, so physically and emotionally tired her limbs felt like dead weights, but in the split second before she fell asleep she acknowledged it wasn't just for the baby she was going to see Miriam tomorrow. It was for Forde too.

* * *

Miriam Cotton wasn't at all what Melanie had expected. For one thing her consulting room was part of her home, a cosy, friendly extension to the original Edwardian terrace overlooking the narrow walled garden consisting of a neat lawn and flowerbeds with an enormous cherry tree in the centre of it. And Miriam herself was something of a revelation, her thick white hair trimmed into an urchin cut with vivid red highlights and her slim figure clothed in jeans and a loose blue shirt. She had a wide smile, big blue eyes and lines where you would expect lines for someone of her age on her clear complexion. Altogether she gave the impression of someone who was at peace with herself. Melanie liked her immediately.

Once sitting in a plump armchair next to the glowing fire—artificial, Miriam informed her cheerfully, but the most realistic Melanie had ever seen—and with no consulting couch, which she had been preparing herself for all day and dreading, Melanie began to relax a little. There was something about Forde's friend's mother that inspired trust.

Miriam smiled at her from the other armchair. 'Before we go any further I must make one thing perfectly clear. Anything we talk about, anything you tell me is strictly between the two of us. Forde is a dear man but he will not be party to anything which is said in this room, not unless you wish to confide in him, of course. You have my absolute word on that.'

'Thank you.' Melanie nodded and relaxed a little more. She didn't want to have any secrets from Forde, it wasn't that, but knowing she still retained some control was nonetheless reassuring. It made her feel safe.

'Forde tells me you're expecting another baby?' Miriam said quietly.

Melanie nodded again. She was glad Miriam had said 'another' and not pretended Matthew hadn't been born. 'Yes, in the spring.' She hesitated. 'I suppose that's the main reason— No.' She paused, shaking her head. 'That's not right. It's *one* of the reasons I'm here. I guess falling for another baby has brought everything to a head.'

'Everything?' Miriam said even more quietly.

Melanie looked into the gentle face opposite her. There were family photographs covering one wall of the room and she had noticed one little girl was in a wheelchair. This woman knew about trouble and heartache, she thought, biting her lower lip. She would have known that even without the photographs. It was in Miriam's eyes. 'Shall—shall I start at the beginning?' she asked. 'My childhood, I mean.'

'That would be good,' Miriam said softly. 'And take your time. You can come to see me here as often as you like, every evening if you wish, until you feel ready to stop. Forde has been a wonderful friend to my son and you take priority right now. All right?'

Melanie left the house at seven o'clock feeling like a wet rag. She, who prided herself on not wearing her heart on her sleeve, had wept and wailed through the last two hours in a manner that horrified her now she thought about it.

She climbed into the pickup, which she'd parked a few metres from Miriam's front door. It looked somewhat incongruous in the line of mostly expensive cars the well-to-do street held, but Melanie didn't notice.

She took several deep breaths before she started the engine. She was far from convinced all this was a good idea, she told herself grimly. She felt worse, much worse if anything, after all the emotion of the last hours. Admittedly Miriam had seemed to guess how she was feeling and had assured her it was the same for everyone initially. She had to persevere to come out of the other end of the dark tunnel, according to Miriam. But what if she got stuck in the tunnel? What then?

She drew out of the parking space into the road, a deep weariness making her limbs feel heavy.

Then she straightened her back and lifted her chin. She had promised Forde and she would keep her end of the bargain. She would come back tomorrow and all the other tomorrows until this thing was done.

Melanie drove home slowly, aware she was totally exhausted and needed to be ultra careful. Once at the cottage she fixed herself a quick meal before falling into bed. She was asleep as soon as her head touched the pillow.

That evening was to set the pattern for the next few weeks, but the morning after her first visit to Miriam she attended the local hospital for her first scan. It was a bittersweet day. She remembered how she and Forde had come together for Matthew's first scan, excited and thrilled as they had waited to see the baby on the monitor, and slightly apprehensive in case everything wasn't as it should be.

This time she sat alone in the waiting area, which was smaller than the one in the hospital in London—her own choice, she reminded herself as she watched the couple in front of her come out of the room where the scan took place wrapped in each other's arms and smiling.

Once she was lying on the bed it was more of a repeat of the time before. The lady taking the scan was smiling; all was well, heartbeat strong, baby developing as it should be and no concerns.

She left the hospital clutching two pictures of the child in her womb and with tears of relief and thankfulness streaming down her face.

Once she was sitting in the truck in the hospital car park she took a few minutes to compose herself before phoning Forde on his mobile. He answered immediately. 'Nell? What's wrong?'

'Nothing's wrong. I've been to the hospital for the first scan and everything's fine with the baby. I just wanted you to know. I've a picture for you. I'll leave it with Isabelle.'

It was a moment before he spoke and his voice was gruff. 'Thank God. And I mean that, thank God. They can't tell if it's a boy or a girl at this stage, can they?'

'No. That's at twenty weeks. Do you want to know?' They hadn't found out with Matthew.

'I don't know. Do you?'

'I'm not sure. I'll ring you near the time and discuss it then. I have to go to work now. Goodbye, Forde.'

His voice was husky when he said, 'Goodbye, Nell.'

It took her another ten minutes to dry her eyes and compose herself again before she could start the truck and drive out of the hospital confines, but by the time she got to Isabelle's house she was in command of herself.

Isabelle insisted on giving her a hot drink before she

joined James in the garden, and her mother-in-law was entranced with the picture of her future grandchild. 'Do you mind if I take a copy of it for myself before I pass this on to Forde tonight?' Isabelle asked as they finished their hot chocolate and custard creams at the kitchen table. 'He's calling in later for dinner. I don't suppose you'd like to stay too?'

Melanie shook her head. 'I'm going to see Miriam again.' She had thought it only right to tell her mother-in-law what she was doing yesterday and now she was glad she had. It was the perfect excuse and had the added bonus of being the truth.

'Is it being nosy if I ask you how it went?' Isabelle said gently.

'Of course not.' Melanie shrugged. 'But I can't give you much of an answer because I'm not sure myself. It was...traumatic, I suppose.'

'But helpful?'

Melanie shrugged again. 'I don't know, Isabelle. I guess time will tell.' She drank the last of her hot chocolate and stood up. 'I'd better go and help James with the planting.'

Once outside, she lifted her face to the silver-grey sky. Helpful. How could anything so painful be helpful? She wasn't looking forward to the next weeks.

November turned into December amid biting white frosts and brilliantly cold days, but she and James managed to complete the work at Isabelle's by the end of the first week of December.

And Forde kept his word. He didn't come to the cottage and he didn't call her. In fact he could have fallen off the edge of the world and she'd be none the wiser, Melanie thought to herself irritably more than once, before taking herself to task for her inconsistency.

Pride had forbidden her to mention him to Isabelle while she had still been working at her mother-in-law's house. It seemed the height of hypocrisy to do so anyway after she had left him and was still refusing to go back. What could she say? Was he well? Was he happy? And after that time when Isabelle had asked her to stay for dinner on the day of the scan, her mother-in-law had talked about everything under the sun except Forde. Which wasn't like Isabelle and led Melanie to suspect her mother-in-law was obeying orders from her son.

She could be wrong, of course, maybe she was being paranoid, but, whatever, she couldn't complain.

But she missed him. Terribly. It had been bad enough when she had first left him in the early part of the year, but then she had been reconciled to the fact her marriage was over. She had thrown herself into making her business work and finding herself a home, and, although that hadn't compensated for not having him around, it had occupied her mind some of the time. Furnishing the cottage, turning her tiny courtyard garden into a small oasis, making sure any professional work she did was done to the best of her ability and drumming up business had all played its part in dulling her mind against the pain.

But now...

Since he had muscled his way into her life again that night in August he'd reopened a door she was powerless to shut. He'd penetrated her mind—and her body, she thought wryly, her hand going to the swell of her belly.

And in spite of herself she wanted to see him, the more so as the sessions with Miriam progressed.

She was finding herself in a strange place emotionally as her deepest fears and anxieties stemming from her troubled childhood and even more troubled teens were unearthed. She had to come to terms with the truth that she'd buried the fact she'd always felt worthless and unloved behind the capable, controlled façade she presented to the world. And as time had gone on something had begun to happen to the solid ball of pain and fear and sorrow lodged in her heart. It had begun to slowly disintegrate, and, though the process wasn't without its own anguish and grief, it was cleansing.

Gradually, very gradually she was beginning to accept the concept that her confusion and despair as a child had coloured her view of herself. She hadn't been responsible for her parents' death or that of her grandmother, or her friend's tragic accident either. None of that had been her fault.

The miscarriage was harder to come to terms with, her grief still frighteningly raw. It helped more than she could ever express that Miriam had pushed aside her professional status and cried with her on those sessions, revealing to Melanie that she'd lost a baby herself at six months and had blamed herself for a long time afterwards.

'It's what we do as women,' Miriam had said wryly as she'd dried her eyes after one particularly harrowing meeting. 'Take the blame, punish ourselves, try to make sense of what is an unexplainable tragedy. But you weren't to blame. You would have given your life for Matthew as I would have given mine for my baby.'

'Forde said that once, that I'd have given my life for Matthew's if I could,' Melanie had said thoughtfully.

'He's right.' Miriam had patted her arm gently. 'And he loves you very much. Lots of women go a whole lifetime without being loved like Forde loves you. You can trust him—you know that, don't you?'

But could she trust herself? She wanted to. More than anything she longed to put the past behind her and believe she could be a good wife and mother and a rational and optimistic human being, but how did she know if she had the strength of mind to do that or would she fall back into the old fears and anxieties that would cripple her and ultimately those she loved?

Melanie was thinking about the conversation with Miriam on the day before Christmas Eve. She was curled up on one of the sofas in her sitting room, which she'd pulled close to the glowing fire, watching an old Christmassy film on TV but without paying it any real attention. She had finished work until after the New Year; the ground had been as hard as iron for weeks and heavy snow was forecast within the next twenty-four hours.

She and James had finished the job they'd gone on to once Isabelle's garden was completed and James had disappeared off to Scotland to spend Christmas with his parents and a whole host of relations, although she suspected it was more the allure of the Hogmanay party his parents always held on New Year's Eve that he didn't want to miss. He had invited her to go with him, telling her his parents' house was always packed full over the festive season and one more would make no difference, but she'd declined the offer. A couple of her friends had invited her for Christmas lunch, and both Isabelle and Miriam had made noises in that direction, but she had politely said no to everyone.

She had forbidden the one person she wanted to spend Christmas with from coming anywhere near her, and although part of her wanted to call Forde and just hear his voice, another part—a stronger part—didn't feel ready for what that might entail. She had bought him a Christmas card and then decided not to send it because for the life of her she couldn't find the right words to say. She knew she would have to phone him after Christmas about the next scan; it was only two weeks away now.

She rested her hand on the mound of her stomach and in response felt a fluttering that made her smile. That had happened several times in the last week and it never failed to thrill her. Her baby, living, growing, moving inside her, a little person who would have its own mind and personality. She had felt this baby move much earlier than she had Matthew but her friends who had children had assured her it was like that with the second. And with each experience of feeling those tiny arms and legs stretching and kicking she had wondered how ever she'd be able to hand their child over to Forde and walk away. It would kill her, she thought, shutting her eyes tightly. But would it be the best thing for her baby? She didn't know any more. She had been so sure before she'd started seeing Miriam, but now, the more she understood herself and what had led her to think that way, the more she'd dared to hope. Hope that maybe, just maybe, the depression that had kicked in after the miscarriage and that had been fed by the insecurities of her past had fooled her into thinking that way.

'You're not a Jonah, Melanie.' Miriam had said that at their last session as they were saying goodbye. 'You are like everyone else. Some people sail through life without encountering any problems, others seem to have loads from day one, but it's all due to chance, unfair though that is. I can't say the rest of your life is going to be a bowl of cherries, no one can, but I *can* say you have a choice right now. You can either look at the negatives and convince yourself it's all doom and gloom, or you can take life by the throat and kick it into submission. Know what I mean?'

'Like Cassie and Sarah?' she'd answered. Sarah was the little girl in a wheelchair in the photograph. She was beautiful, with curly brown hair and huge, limpid green eyes, but she had been born with spina bifida and other medical complications. Cassie, her mother, was devoted to her and in the summer Cassie had been diag-nosed with multiple sclerosis, but according to Miriam her daughter was determined to fight her illness every inch of the way. Sarah, young as she was, had the same spirit, her proud grandmother said, and was a joy to be with. Miriam had admitted to Melanie she'd cried bitter tears over them both but would never dream of letting her daughter or granddaughter know because neither of them 'did' self-pity.

'My Cassie must have had her down times over Sarah and now this multiple sclerosis has reared its head, but, apart from in the early days with Sarah just after she was born, I've never seen Cassie anything but positive.'

Miriam had looked at her, her eyes soft. 'You can be like that, Melanie. I know it.'

A log fell further into the glowing ash, sending a shower of sparks up the chimney. It roused Melanie from her thoughts and she glanced at the dwindling stack of logs and empty coal scuttle. She must go and bring more logs in and fill the scuttle before it got dark, she thought, rising to her feet reluctantly. James had helped her build a lean-to in her small paved front garden in the summer for her supply of logs and sacks of coal. She hadn't wanted to lose any space in her tiny private courtyard at the back of the property, and as the front of the properties only overlooked a local farmer's hay barns there was no one to object. Nevertheless, they had taken care to give the lean-to a quaint, rustic look in keeping with the cottages and as one side was enclosed by her neighbour's high wooden fence it kept her fuel relatively dry and protected.

When she opened the front door an icy blast of air hit her and the sky looked grey and low although it was only three in the afternoon. She filled the scuttle to the weight she was happy to carry now she was pregnant and took it inside, before going back for some logs. She took an armful in and then went back for some more, and it was only then she noticed a slight movement close to the fence behind the stack of wood.

Petrified it was a rat—one or two of the neighbours had mentioned seeing the odd rat or two, courtesy of the farmer's barns, no doubt—Melanie hurried back inside the house, her heart pounding like a drum. As soon as she had closed the door she knew she had to go back and make sure what it was, though. What if a bird had somehow got trapped or some other creature was hurt? Situated as the cottages were in a small hamlet surrounded by countryside, it could be anything sheltering there.

Wishing with all her heart she hadn't gone out for the logs and coal and were still sitting watching TV in front of the fire, she put on a coat before opening the door again. The temperature seemed to have dropped another few degrees in just a minute or two. There was no doubt excited children all over the country were going to get their wish of a white Christmas, she thought, treading carefully to where she'd seen the movement. She bent down, her muscles poised to spring away if a beady-eyed rodent jumped out at her.

But it wasn't a rat that stared back at her. Squeezed into the tiniest space possible, a small tabby cat crouched shivering in its makeshift shelter, all huge amber eyes and trembling fur.

'Why, hello,' Melanie whispered softly, putting out her hand only for the cat to shrink back as far as it could. 'Hey, I'm not going to hurt you. Don't be frightened. Come on, puss.'

After several minutes of murmuring sweet nothings, by which time she was shaking with cold as much as the cat, Melanie realised she was getting nowhere. She could also see the cat was all bone under its fur but with a distended stomach, which either meant it was pregnant or had some kind of growth. Praying it was the former because she was already consumed with pity for the poor little mite, she stood up and went to fetch some cooked roast chicken from the kitchen, hoping to tempt it with food where gentle encouragement had failed.

The cat was clearly starving, but not starving enough to leave its sanctuary, roast chicken or no roast chicken.

'I can't leave you out here. Please, please come out,' Melanie begged, close to tears. It was getting darker by the minute and the wind was cutting through her like a knife, but the thought of abandoning the cat to its fate just wasn't an option. And if she started to move the pile of logs it was sheltering behind they might fall and crush the little thing. She had tried reaching a hand to it but was a couple of inches short of being able to grab it.

'Nell? What the hell are you doing out here and who are you talking to?' said Forde's voice behind her.

She swung round and there he was. Whether it was because she was frozen or had moved too quickly or was faint with relief that he was here to help her, she didn't know, but the next thing she knew there was a rushing in her ears and from her crouched position beside the cat she slid onto her bottom, struggling with all her might not to pass out as the darkness moved from the sky into her head and became overwhelming.

CHAPTER TEN

IN THE end Melanie didn't lose consciousness. She was aware of Forde kneeling beside her and holding her against him as he told her to take deep breaths and stay still—not that she could have done anything else. She was also aware of the wonderful smell and feel of him—big, solid, breathtakingly reassuring. It was when he tried to lift her into his arms, saying, 'I'm taking you indoors,' that she found her voice.

'No. No, you can't. There's a cat, Forde. It's in trouble,' she muttered weakly.

'A cat?' The note of incredulity in his voice would have been comical under other circumstances. 'What are you talking about? You're frozen, woman. I'm taking you in.'

'No.' Her voice was stronger now and she pushed his arms away when he tried to gather her up. 'There *is* a cat, behind the wood there, and it's ill or pregnant or both. Look, see for yourself.' She allowed him to help her to her feet but wouldn't budge an inch, saying again, 'Look, there. And I can't reach it and it's terrified, Forde. We can't leave it out here in this weather—'

'All right, all right.' Thoroughly exasperated but less panicked now she was on her feet and seemingly OK,

Forde peered into the shadows where she was pointing. At first he thought she must be imagining things and then he saw it—a little scrap of nothing crouched behind the logs. 'Yes, I see it. Are you sure it won't just come out and go home once we leave it alone?'

Her voice held all the controlled patience women drew on when the male of the species said something outrageously stupid. 'Quite sure, Forde. And I don't think it has a home to go to. Whatever's happened to it, it isn't good. The thing's absolutely scared stiff of humans, can't you see? And it's starving.'

Forde narrowed his eyes as he tried to see in what was rapidly becoming pitch blackness. 'It looks plump enough to me,' he said eventually. 'In fact quite rotund.'

'That's its belly. The rest of it is skeletal, for goodness' sake. We have to do something.'

'Right.' In a way he was grateful to the cat. He'd come here tonight because he'd heard the weather was going to get atrocious and it was the excuse he'd been looking for to see her for weeks. While she'd gone to see Miriam as promised he hadn't wanted to do anything to rock the boat, and her demands had been very explicit—no contact. But, he had reasoned to himself on the drive from London, she could hardly object to him calling to see if she was well stocked up with provisions and ready for the blizzard that had been forecast for some days. He'd bought half of his local delicatessen just in case, as well as a few other luxuries he could blame on the festive season. He'd been hoping she would be mellow enough to ask him in for a drink, but he hadn't expected to be welcomed with open arms like this—even if it was due to a homeless moggy. But beggars couldn't be choosers.

'What are you going to do?' she said. 'We have to help it.'

He glanced at her. She was literally wringing her hands. Feeling that chances like this didn't come that often, he gestured towards the cottage. 'Go and open the door and get ready to close it again once I get the thing in the house.'

'But you won't *reach* it,' she almost wailed.

'I'll reach it.' If there was a God, he'd reach it. Once she was in position in the doorway to the cottage, he reached into the narrow void between the fence and the logs. He heard the cat hiss and spit before he felt its claws but somehow he got it by the scruff of the neck and hauled it out so he could get a firm hold. He realised immediately Melanie was right, the poor thing was emaciated apart from its swollen stomach, which, if he was right, was full of kittens.

He had grown up with cats and a couple of dogs and now he held the animal against the thick wool of his coat talking soothingly to it and trying not to swear as it used its claws again. But it hadn't bit him. Which, in the circumstances, was something. Especially as it was frightened to death.

Melanie was all fluster once they had got it into the house and shut the door but he still held onto the cat, which had become quieter. 'Nell, warm a little milk in a saucer, and we'll need some food.' He sat down on one of the breakfast bar stools, holding the cat gently but firmly. 'Have you got a cardboard box we could use as a bed for it?'

She shook her head as she slopped milk into a saucer and then began to chop some chicken up. 'I can fetch a blanket if you like? I've several in the airing cupboard.'

'Anything.' The cat had calmed right down but was still shaking. He loosed one of his hands enough to begin stroking it and to his surprise it didn't squirm or try to escape, but lay on his lap as though it was spent. Which it probably was, he thought pityingly. How long it had been fending for itself was anyone's guess, but it hadn't done very well by the look of it. He could imagine it had been a pet that had got pregnant and—with Christmas coming up and all the expense—had become expendable to its delightful owners.

Melanie brought the saucer of milk over and held it in front of the cat as it lay on his lap. It took seconds to finish the lot. Her voice thick with tears, she said, 'The poor thing, Forde. How could someone dump a pretty little cat like this?'

So she had come to the same conclusion as him. 'Beyond me, but I'd like five minutes alone with them,' he said grimly. 'Try the chicken now. I don't want to put it down yet in case it bolts and we frighten it trying to catch it again.'

The chicken went the same way as the milk. Opening his coat, he slipped the cat against the warmth of his cashmere jumper and half closed the edges of the coat around it, making a kind of cocoon. 'It needs to warm up,' he said to Melanie, 'and holding it like this is emphasising we don't mean it any harm. That's more important than anything right now.'

'Shall I get some more milk and chicken?' she asked, putting out a tentative hand and gently stroking the little striped head. The cat tensed for a moment and then relaxed again. It was clearly exhausted.

'No, we don't want to give it too much too quickly and make it sick if it's been without food for a while. Leave it for an hour or two and then we'll try again.'

She nodded, her hand dropping away. Then she looked him straight in the eyes and said honestly, 'I've never been so glad to see anyone in my life. I didn't know what to do.'

Anyone. Not him specifically. But again, better than nothing. He grinned. 'I left my white steed in the car park but it's good to know I can still warm a fair maiden's heart. Talking of which, there's various bits and pieces in the car I need to fetch in a while.'

'Bits and pieces?'

'I wanted to make sure you were stocked up with provisions in view of the snow that's coming.' Considering how well he'd done with the moggy he thought he could push his luck. 'And I was hoping we could perhaps share a meal?' he added with a casualness that didn't quite come off. 'Before I go back?'

Melanie's big brown eyes surveyed him solemnly. 'That would be lovely,' she said simply.

The cat chose that moment to begin purring and Forde knew exactly how it felt. To hide the surge of elation he'd felt at her words, he smiled, saying, 'Listen to that. This is a nice cat. In spite of what's happened to it it's still prepared to trust us.'

'I'll make us a coffee. It's decaf now, I'm afraid.'

'Decaf's fine.' Mud mixed with water would have been fine right at that moment.

He drank the coffee with the cat still nestled against

him, now fast asleep. They talked of inconsequential things, both carefully feeling their way. Outside the wind grew stronger, howling like a banshee and rattling the windows.

After a while Melanie fetched a blanket from her little airing cupboard and they made a bed for the cat in her plastic laundry basket. They fed it more milk and chicken before Forde gently extracted it from his coat and laid it in the basket, whereupon it went straight to sleep again. Melanie had placed the basket next to the radiator in the kitchen and it was as warm as toast.

'It's still a very young cat,' said Forde as they stood looking down at the little scrap, 'but those are definitely kittens in there and if I'm not much mistaken she's due pretty soon.'

'How soon?' Melanie showed her alarm. She liked animals but she had never had much to do with any while growing up. As for the mechanics of a cat giving birth...

'Hard to tell. Could be hours, could be days.'

'But time enough to get her to a vet?'

'That might freak her out.' Forde was thinking. 'How far is your nearest vet?'

Melanie stared at him blankly. 'I've absolutely no idea.'

'OK. Look in the telephone directory while I get the stuff in from the car and find a local vet. It's—' he glanced at his watch '—getting on for five o'clock but they should still be working. I'll give them a ring and ask if someone can come and make a house call.'

'Would they do that if they don't know us?' Melanie asked doubtfully. 'It's not as if we're clients, is it?'

'We won't know that till we ask.'

Without thinking about it she reached up and looped her arms round his neck, kissing him hard and then stepping back a pace before he could respond.

He stared at her, clearly taken aback. 'What was that for?'

'For caring.'

'About the moggy?'

'No, not just the cat,' she said softly.

Something told him not to push it at this stage. 'I'll get the food in. You find that number.'

When he called the veterinary surgery, which was situated some fifteen miles away in the nearest small market town, the receptionist was less than helpful, although she did eventually let him speak to one of the vets after Forde wouldn't take no for an answer. As luck would have it, the woman was young, newly qualified and enthusiastic, added to which Forde used his considerable charm along with offering to pay the call-out fee with his credit card over the telephone and any further costs with cash before she left the cottage.

But Melanie, listening to Forde's end of the exchange, was quite convinced it was the charm that had swung it when the vet said she would be with them within the hour.

Once she began to unpack the bags Forde had brought in she could hardly believe the amount of food he'd bought. A whole cooked ham, a small turkey, a tray of delicious looking canapés, a mulled-cranberry-and-apple-chutney-topped pork pie, cheese of all descriptions, jars of preserves, a Santa-topped Christmas cake and a box of chocolate cup cakes, mince pies, vegetables, nuts, fruit, and still the list went on.

'Forde, this would feed a family of four for a week,' she said weakly when the last bag was empty. 'There's only me. Whatever possessed you?'

'I must have known you'd have a visitor.' He smiled at her over the heaped breakfast bar as she began to stuff what she could in her fridge.

'A visitor?' She glanced at him, colour in her cheeks.

He nodded towards the sleeping cat.

'Oh, yes, of course, but she's hardly going to eat much,' she said flusteredly. For a minute she'd thought… But no, he wouldn't invite himself to stay, not after the rules she'd made. If she wanted him to spend Christmas with her she would have to ask him. But did she want that? Or, more precisely, did she want what that would mean in the days after Christmas and beyond? Because one thing was for sure: she couldn't play fast and loose with his heart any more. She had to be sure. And she wasn't; she wasn't sure. Was she?

'You'd be surprised. She's going to have kittens to feed and she's got lost time to make up for.'

And as though on cue the cat woke up, stretching as she opened big amber eyes and then stood up amid the folds of the blanket. When Forde lifted her out of the laundry basket she didn't struggle but gave a small miaow. Melanie quickly warmed more milk and cut more chicken, and this time Forde set the little animal on its feet to eat. She cleared both saucers, stretched again and then walked over to her makeshift bed and jumped in, settling herself down by kneading the blanket how she wanted it. Then she looked at them.

Melanie knelt down beside her, stroking the brindled fur beneath which she could feel every bone. 'She's so beautiful,' she murmured softly, 'and so brave. She must have been desperate, knowing her babies are going to be born and she had no shelter, no food. It's a wonder she's survived this long.'

A steady, rhythmic vibration began under her fingers as the little cat began to purr; it made her want to cry. How could anyone treat this friendly little creature so cruelly? To throw her out in the winter when they must have known her chances of survival and those of the kittens was poor?

'But now she's found you,' Forde said quietly. 'And she knows she can trust you to look after her.'

Flooded by emotions as turbulent as the weather outside, Melanie looked up at him. She felt as though she were standing at the brink of something profound. 'Do you think I should keep her?'

He didn't prevaricate or throw the ball back in her court. 'Yes, I do. She needs someone to love her unconditionally.'

Melanie blinked back tears. 'But she's so fragile and thin. I can't see her surviving giving birth, Forde. And what of the kittens? If their mother's been starving, what shape will they be in when they're born?'

'Take it a moment by moment, hour by hour. She might surprise you. I think she's a tougher little cookie than she looks. Don't give up on her yet.'

'I'm not about to give up on her,' said Melanie, a trifle indignantly. 'That's the last thing I would do.'

'Good.' He smiled. 'In that case she has a fighting chance.'

The ringing of the doorbell ended further conversation. The vet turned out to be a big, buxom woman with rosy cheeks and large hands, but she was gentleness itself with her small patient. The cat submitted to her ministrations with surprising docility and when she had finished examining her, the vet shook her head. 'I'd be surprised if she's more than a year or so old. She's little more than a kitten herself. That's not good for a number of reasons. She might find it difficult giving birth and in her state she hasn't got any physical strength to fall back on. Being so malnourished I don't know if she would be able to produce a good quality of milk for the kittens, should she or them survive the birth. But—' she looked at them both '—she's a dear little cat, isn't she?'

'What can you do to help in the short term?' Forde asked quietly. 'We want to give her every chance.'

'The main thing she needs is rest and food and food and rest. Have you got a litter tray so she doesn't need to go outside? It's important to keep her warm.'

Forde shook his head. 'But I can get one.'

'Not at this time of night. Follow me back to the surgery and I'll give you one of ours, along with a food made specially for pregnant females and feeding mothers. I'll give her a vitamin injection now and once she's a little stronger she'll need various vaccinations for cat flu and other diseases. I don't want to tax her system by doing that now, and as long as you keep her confined to the house for the time being she won't come into contact with other felines who might be carrying diseases. I think she's due very soon, although it's difficult to tell in a case like this. If she does begin and you're worried for any reason, call me. I'll give you my mobile number.'

She smiled. 'Having done that we can almost guarantee she'll start as I sit down for my Christmas lunch.'

'That's very good of you,' said Melanie.

'This is an exceptional case,' the young woman said quietly. 'I hate to think what she's been through in the last weeks. Now, let her eat and drink little and often in the next twenty-four hours and try to get as much down her as she wants. But I have to warn you—' again she glanced at them both '—the odds are stacked against her giving birth to live kittens. I can give you vitamin drops to put in her food but I'm afraid it might well be too little too late.'

Melanie nodded. 'Nevertheless, we want to try.'

'Good. Fuss her, talk to her and give her plenty of TLC. You won't read that in any veterinary journal but in my opinion it works wonders with animals that have been ill treated. They understand far more than we give them credit for.'

The vet gave them a few more instructions and then she and Forde left, leaving Melanie with Tabitha, as she had decided to call the pretty little animal. She found she was on tenterhooks all the time Forde was gone. Forde had carried the basket into the sitting room for her before he departed, setting it on the thick rug in front of the fire, and after a little more food Tabitha had gone soundly asleep. Melanie tried to watch TV but her whole attention was fixed on the sleeping feline.

The vet had run through the signs to look for when the cat started labour and what to expect, and Melanie found herself praying the whole time nothing would happen before Forde got back. He'd know what to do; he always did.

The relief she felt when she heard him call to her when he let himself in with the key she'd given him was overwhelming. She flew out into the hall, her words tumbling over themselves as she said, 'Did you get everything? Should we try and give her some of the special food right now? Where should we put the litter tray? Do you think she'll let us know when she needs to use it?' She stopped to draw breath.

Forde regarded her with amused eyes. 'Yes, yes, litter tray by the basket and maybe.'

He looked big and dark and impossibly attractive in her tiny hall, and sexy. Incredibly sexy. Before she knew what she was saying, she blurted, 'Will you stay here tonight, in case something happens?'

He smiled a sweet smile. 'I didn't intend to leave you by yourself, Nell. Now, we'll get our patient organised with some more food and then we'll eat ourselves, OK? Ham and eggs, something quick and easy. Have you got a spare duvet I can use tonight and perhaps a pillow for the sofa?'

'You'll never sleep on my sofas.' His long frame was double their length. 'I can stay down here with her.'

'You need your sleep.' He glanced at the swell of her stomach under the soft Angora sweater-dress she was wearing. 'And I'll be fine. Now, let's see how she likes this food compared to the chicken.'

The food smelt quite disgusting when they opened the tin, the odour of fish overpowering, but Tabitha finished a saucerful without seemingly pausing for breath.

'Cat caviar,' commented Forde drily. 'It should be too, considering the price. Remind me to come out of property developing and into cat food.'

Melanie smiled. It was scarily good having him here. And not just because of Tabitha.

They ate their own meal at the dining-room table. Melanie was glad she'd cleared it of paperwork a few days before and put a festive centrepiece of holly with bright red berries in pride of place. That, along with her small, fragrant Christmas tree decorated with baubles and tinsel in the sitting room and the cards dotted about, gave the impression she'd made some effort. In truth, she'd never felt less like celebrating Christmas. Or it had been that way until she had heard Forde's voice.

Melanie had insisted on having Tabitha's basket where they could see her while they ate, and after they'd finished the meal she carried their decaf coffee and the chocolate cup cakes Forde had bought through to the sitting room, while Forde brought Tabitha. The little cat looked out serenely from the basket as Forde set it in front of the fire again, apparently quite happy with all the coming and going.

The cup cakes were heavenly. Melanie ate three, one after another, and then looked at Forde aghast. 'I'm going to be as big as a house before this baby's born. Now the sickness has gone all I think about is food. I no sooner eat breakfast than I'm thinking about lunch and then dinner, and Christmas doesn't help with all the extra temptations of cake and plum pudding and chocolate.'

'Nell, you could never look anything but gorgeous to me.' He lifted her small chin, licking a smear of chocolate icing from the corner of her mouth before kissing her as though no one else in the world existed. Her lips, as soft and warm as mulled wine, moved against his and she kissed him back, her hands sliding up to his shoulders and tangling in his hair.

He caught the moan that fluttered in her throat with his breath, his kiss deepening still more and his tongue beginning an insistent probing that brought every nerve in her body to singing life. Before she knew what he was doing he had moved and lifted her so she was sitting on his lap. Now his mouth moved from her lips to trail a burning path to her throat and down into the V of her cleavage.

Melanie gasped and he lifted her head to look into her flushed face. 'I want you,' he murmured softly, 'all the time. At my desk when I'm working, in the car, at home when I'm eating a meal or taking a shower. There's not a minute of a day when I'm not thinking about you. You're in my blood, do you know that? For life. A sweet addiction that's impossible to fight.'

'Do you want to fight it?' she asked faintly, his silvery eyes mesmerising.

His mouth twisted in a bittersweet smile. 'There have been times when I've thought the pain would be easier if I did, but, no, I don't.'

This time she kissed him and his body throbbed with the contact. His hands ran over her breasts, the soft wool beneath his fingers moulding to the rounded globes and her nipples hard and engorged. She didn't object when he tugged her dress upwards, helping him by lifting her arms as he pulled it over her head. Her lacy bra showed her breasts were fuller and her cleavage deeper, the firm mound of her belly making his breath catch in his throat. Her body was changing, to accommodate his son or daughter. The surge of possessive love expanded his chest and made it difficult to breathe.

'Forde?'

'You're so beautiful, Nell,' he whispered, his eyes brilliant with unshed tears. 'So beautiful.'

They undressed each other slowly and completely, touching and tasting as they did so until they were both naked and trembling with desire. Then she climbed on top of him on the sofa where they were lying, sitting astride him as she lowered herself onto the proud rod of his erection.

Her body was warm, unbelievably soft and welcoming as it accepted him, and as she began to move he struggled to keep control so she was fulfilled along with him. He could see the pleasure in her face and it was almost more erotic than he could bear, his body shaking as his muscles clenched against the release it was aching for.

He felt her climax and went with her, their sanity shattering into pure sensation and then reforming in the aftermath of drugged passion. It was a few moments after she had snuggled against him before either of them could speak. 'Wow,' murmured Forde huskily. 'Tell me this isn't a dream and I'm going to wake up in a minute back at the house.'

'It's real.' She shivered as she spoke and he reached for the throw hanging over the back of the sofa, wrapping it round them as she settled her head on his chest. Within moments she was fast asleep, just the odd spit and crackle from the fire disturbing the pine-scented stillness. He glanced at the basket. The cat was sleeping too amid the folds of the blanket, its small striped body barely moving with each breath.

I owe you, Forde told it silently. *And now you've got me this far I'm not leaving.*

The room was all dancing shadows, the flickering flames of the fire and the lights on Melanie's Christmas tree creating a soothing, womblike feeling. Outside the wind continued to moan and howl, and now sleet was hurling itself against the windows with a ferocity that made the room even warmer and cosier in comparison to the storm outside.

Holding Melanie close, he shut his eyes.

CHAPTER ELEVEN

A DISTANT vibration brought Melanie out of a satisfying dream. She opened sleepy eyes to find she was lying with her cheek on Forde's hairy chest and with her body snuggled into his side like a little animal burying itself into the source of its comfort, his heartbeat still echoing in her head. She didn't let herself think for a few moments, relishing the feel and smell of him and the fact that he was here, with her. The baby moved, the flutterings the strongest yet, as though it knew its father was close.

And then she smiled to herself at such fanciful imaginings.

She raised her head carefully to look at Tabitha, aware she and Forde must have slept for an hour or more, but the cat was still sound asleep. The vet had said the best medicine for her was food and rest; if only they could make sure she had a few days of both before she delivered her kittens they might all make it, along with their mother. *Please, please, God, let this be a happy ending,* she prayed silently. *I want a happy ending for once. She's only a little cat—don't take her before her life has really begun. And the kittens, let them live to grow and play and feel the sun on their fur in the summer. Please.*

Forde had said Tabitha knew she could trust them to look after her, that she needed someone to love her unconditionally. She knew now why his words had struck such a chord in her. It was how Forde was with her; from the day they had met he had put her needs before his, in the bedroom and out of it, and his love had been unlimited and without reservation.

She drew in a shuddering breath, her mind clearer than it had been for months.

After Matthew had died her guilt and remorse had turned her mind and heart inwards. She'd been so wrapped up in her own culpability and self-condemnation, so convinced she was a jinx and that Forde would be better off without her, that she hadn't considered she might be wrong. She'd been too self-centred. Wrapped up in her own grief, she hadn't taken on board he was suffering too, not really, not as she should have. She had learnt a lot about herself over the last weeks with Miriam, and some of it had been hard to take.

But Forde didn't see her as she saw herself. He loved her. Utterly. Absolutely. As he'd told her to love Tabitha—unconditionally. When she had left him he had told her he would never let her go, that she could divorce him, flee to the other side of the world, refuse to see or talk to him, but he would never give up trying to make her see sense and come back to him. It had panicked her then, terrified her even. But now...

She raised her head and stared at his sleeping face.

Now she was humbly and eternally grateful. Her

hand went to the swell of her belly wherein their child lay. And she could never walk away from her baby and its father. How could she have considered such a possibility even for a moment? But deep inside she'd always known she wouldn't have the strength to give her baby up. That had been what had *really* frightened her once she'd known she was pregnant, because then she had still believed she was a curse on those she loved.

And now? a little voice outside herself asked insistently. What did she believe now? Because if she went back to Forde it had to be with all her body, soul and spirit. She'd asked for a happy ending for Tabitha but she had to believe in one for herself. Believe she could trust Forde implicitly, give him that little part of herself she had always kept back. Could she do that?

She heard a scratching sound and raised her head again. Tabitha was awake and turning round and round in the basket and Melanie could have sworn there was a faintly worried expression on the cat's delicate face. Tabitha gave a little cry that was more of a yowl than a miaow, and then jumped out of the basket and disappeared behind the other sofa.

Oh, no. Melanie sat bolt upright and in so doing woke Forde, who mumbled dazedly, 'What the… Nell?'

'I think Tabitha's going to have her kittens.' Even to herself her voice sounded thick with fear. 'It's too soon, Forde. I wanted her to have some days of good food and rest. What are we going to do?'

Forde sat up, swinging his feet onto the carpet and raking back his hair. 'Where is she?' he asked, eyeing the empty basket.

'Behind the other sofa. The vet said she might hide.'

He stood up naked as the day he was born and walked across the room, peering over the back of the sofa. Damn it, Nell was right. The cat was behaving exactly as the vet had warned it might. They had all been hoping they could have a few days of feeding her up but it looked as if time had run out.

He turned, gathering up Melanie's scattered clothes along with his own. 'We can do very little now except keep an eye on her. The rest is up to Tabitha. I'll move the basket behind the sofa if that's where she wants to be. Get dressed and go and make us a hot drink. This could take a while.'

'It's too soon,' Melanie said again, her old fears and doubts resurfacing in a flood.

Forde reached out a hand and stroked her cheek for a moment. 'Stop panicking. Tabitha will pick up on it. Animals are incredibly sensitive that way. Bring some warm milk and food in for her when you get our drinks, OK? Now get dressed, there's a good girl.'

Once in the kitchen Melanie realised the icy sleet had turned into snow while she and Forde had been sleeping and already it was a couple of inches thick. The swirling flakes were fat and feathery and the sky was laden. If the storm continued in its present form she doubted if the vet would be able to get through to them if they needed her.

She stood for a moment, eyes wide and her top lip clamped in her teeth before telling herself to get on with what she had to do. Tabitha would be all right. Anything else wasn't an option. And the kittens would be fine too. They had to be.

Tabitha drank the milk they slid in to her in her hiding place but wouldn't touch the food, and as the yowls increased in volume Melanie had to force herself to sit still and not pace the room. Forde went out to fetch more logs and coal at one point and when he returned, Melanie said simply, 'I know,' in answer to the look on his face regarding the weather.

Forde had resorted to lying on the floor and peering under the sofa by the time the first kitten was born some three hours later. Tabitha had ignored the basket at the side of her but she dealt expertly with the tiny thing, biting off the birth sac and beginning to lick it all over with her abrasive tongue. When Forde saw it squirm he experienced a profound relief, more for Melanie than the cat.

Another kitten was born fairly quickly, and as they watched Tabitha begin the same procedure with this one as she had with the first Melanie whispered, 'Look at that, Forde. She's going to be a brilliant mother. And the kittens are alive and well.'

He looked at her where she lay at the side of him on the carpet. He'd been about to warn her that it was early days yet, that a hundred and one things could go wrong. There were more kittens to be born and they might not be as lucky as the first two, and Tabitha herself might be too exhausted to survive much more of this. But then he looked into her deep brown eyes and something in them checked his words. Instead he put his hand on hers.

There followed a wait that seemed endless to Melanie and Forde. They hardly dared move from their vigil but then a third kitten made its appearance and once again Tabitha went into action. This time, though, once the kitten was cleaned up to its mother's satisfaction, Tabitha picked up the tiny creature and jumped into the laundry basket where she deposited the squirming little scrap before fetching the other two, one by one, to the place she deemed as safe. She then made short work of the food and fresh milk Forde had slid under the sofa next to the basket and joined her kittens after using the litter tray.

'Do you think that's it? There were just the three?' Melanie found she had a crick in her neck and was utterly exhausted. She was also more elated than words could have described.

'Looks like it.' Forde was trying not to reveal how relieved he was that things had gone so well. Tabitha seemed to have taken the whole process in her stride despite her poor state of health and the kittens had wriggled to their mother's teats like homing pigeons. He also blessed the fact that Mother Nature had seen fit to give the little cat just three kittens to cope with. They stood a far better chance than if it had been a large litter. They hadn't been able to see clearly what the kittens looked like, their view had been restricted, but the fact that the little animals were sleek and damp from their mother's ministrations meant they really didn't look like cats at all.

'What do we do now?' Melanie sat up and stretched her aching neck. 'I don't like the thought of leaving her alone.'

'Looks like Tabitha's ready for a well-earned rest.' Forde stood up and pulled her to her feet. 'You get off to bed and I'll sleep with one eye open down here.'

Melanie looked at her husband. This had to come from her. She knew that. 'Or you could carry the basket upstairs and put it near the radiator in the bedroom so we could be on hand if she needs us? We could take some milk and food up with us and put it near the basket in case she's hungry in the night.'

Forde looked at her, a look with a deep searching question colouring it.

'I—I don't want to sleep alone for one more night,' she whispered. 'I was wrong about so many things, Forde. I knew that deep down, I guess, but seeing Miriam allowed everything to be brought into the light of day, all the doubts and fears. I—I want us to be together, not just for Christmas but for the rest of our lives and—'

She didn't get any further before she was lifted right off her feet and into his arms. He kissed her as if there were no tomorrow and she kissed him back in the same way, clinging to him so tightly he could hardly breathe.

Setting her down after a long minute, he drew her over to the sofa and then sat her on his lap. 'Are you sure?' he said softly. 'That all the doubts and fears are gone, I mean?'

He deserved the truth. She touched his face with the side of her palm. 'I want to be,' she said honestly. 'And I know myself so much better now, but I guess to some extent I'm still a work in progress. I was so scared tonight, with Tabitha.'

'Nell, so was I. That's natural.' He kissed her hard on her lips. 'It goes hand in hand with love, the worry and the fear that you'll lose the beloved. It's the other side of the coin, I suppose. But the best side makes it worth coping with the flip side—know what I mean?' He kissed her again. 'And most of the time the best side is uppermost. You had a rough start to life and you developed a defence mechanism to keep people at arm's length so you couldn't be hurt and you couldn't hurt them. I understand that. And then I came along and everything changed. If things had been different with Matthew you would still have had to face the fact, sooner or later, that you needed to unearth some of the issues you'd buried way deep inside. But it would have happened slowly, more naturally.'

'But the miscarriage did happen. Matthew died.' It still hurt as much as ever to stay it and she wondered if that would ever change. But the nature of the grief had changed subtly over the last weeks. It was still as intense but more bearable because the crucifying guilt had gone. She could mourn her perfect, exquisite little boy without feeling she had to punish herself every second of every day.

'Yes, he died.' There was a wealth of emotion in Forde's voice. 'And there will always be regrets, especially because with an accident of that nature there are so many ifs and buts in hindsight. You aren't the only one who blamed yourself. I knew you weren't too good that day. I could have stayed home with you. What does work matter compared to you and our son? And Janet had her own self-reproaches too. She wished she'd stayed with you while you ate and then brought the tray down, but none of us *knew*.'

Melanie nodded. How many times had she longed to turn back the clock until the morning of the accident so she could have done things differently? Too many to count. She had relived every minute of that fateful morning until she'd thought she was losing her mind. It had to stop. Once and for all, it had to stop. She had to be strong for this baby and for Forde, and for Matthew too. He had a right to be remembered with passionate love and devotion, and, yes, with a certain amount of pain too, but the memory of her precious baby son had been in danger of being marred and destroyed by her corrosive guilt.

'He was so beautiful,' she whispered through her tears.

'And so tiny.' Forde's voice was husky. 'He weighed nothing at all in my arms.'

She rested her forehead against his as their tears mingled, but for the first time since Matthew had died they were healing tears. After a long time when they just held each other close, she said softly, 'I love you. I have always loved you and I always will. I want you to know that. You are the other part of me, the better part.'

'Never that.' He kissed her fiercely. 'You are perfect in every way to me, never forget that. And I will never hurt you, Nell. I might get it wrong at times, I might even drive you crazy now and again but I will never hurt you. We will have our children—' he rested his hand on her stomach for a moment '—and grandchildren too, God willing, and grow old together. How does that sound?'

'Pretty good.' She smiled dreamily at him but then her stomach spoilt the moment by rumbling so loudly that Forde chuckled. 'I can't help it,' she protested. 'I haven't eaten for hours and I'm hungry again.'

'How about if you go and get ready for bed and I'll bring us up some supper?' Forde suggested. 'And tomorrow we have a lazy morning. Breakfast in bed, maybe even lunch in bed.'

'You missed out elevenses.'

'That too.' He grinned at her, feeling slightly light-headed that the last nightmarish months were over. He had come here this afternoon with no expectations beyond that they might share a meal together before he drove home. He'd hoped, of course. Hoped that Melanie seeing Miriam might have made a difference, that with the baby coming she would see it had two parents who loved each other and shouldn't be apart, but he hadn't known how long it would take before she conquered her gremlins. But it *was* Christmas after all, a time of miracles...

They ate a hodgepodge of a supper, which Forde brought up on a tray for them to share after he'd installed Tabitha and her kittens by the bedroom radiator in the basket. Wedges of bread from a crusty loaf, slices of fragrant ham, some of the canapés and cheeses he'd bought and slivers of the pork pie, and a couple of enormous pieces of Christmas cake. Curled up close to him in her bed with the snow falling thickly outside and Tabitha fast asleep in the basket, her kittens snuggled into their mother's warm fur, Melanie thought it was the best meal she had ever had.

Afterwards, sated and replete, they made love again, slowly and sensually, the earlier urgency gone. She went to sleep lying in his arms as he held her close to his heart, feeling she wanted this night to last for ever. In a few hours her life had changed beyond recognition, and she had felt closer to Forde as they had made love than she had ever done in the past. Maybe it was because they had come through the fiery trial and were the stronger for it, she thought drowsily, or perhaps for the first time she had met him as an equal partner in her mind and emotions and had kept nothing back. Her guard was lowered and her defences were down, and because of that she could set aside every inhibition.

She opened her eyes one last time to check on Tabitha and the kittens, smiling as she saw three tiny shapes busy feeding. Now the kittens' fur was dry it had fluffed up and they actually looked like baby cats. One appeared to have lighter colouring than the other two but as the room was dimly lit it was hard to see them in the half-light. But all three seemed to be doing well, although, of course, it was early days.

They had to live, she told herself, shutting her eyes and nestling into Forde's body warmth. Tabitha had been remarkable and so brave. After all she'd gone through the little cat had to have the satisfaction of rearing her babies.

She already knew she was going to keep Tabitha and all three kittens. Their house in Kingston upon Thames had a large garden just perfect for four cats; she could already picture the kittens playing and chasing each other across the lawns and shrubbery and climbing the trees. And in the summer all four could lie in the sun together or find a cool place in the shade. Tabitha would never know what it was to be hungry again, she vowed as she drifted off to sleep. Or unloved and unwanted. Not while she had breath in her body.

Melanie awoke on Christmas Eve morning to being kissed deeply and passionately. She opened heavy-lidded eyes to a room full of white light and Forde, clad in nothing but her kitchen apron, smiling at her.

'Your breakfast tray, ma'am.' He indicated a tray holding a full English breakfast, toast and preserves and a glass of orange juice on the bedside table. 'Is there anything else madam would like?'

She would never have dreamt in a million years that a fairly ordinary plastic apron could turn into something so erotic. Remembering the events of the evening before, she raised herself onto her elbow. 'Tabitha?'

'Fed and happy and downstairs by the kitchen radiator again with her three offspring, who are all doing extremely well. I had a nasty moment when I first woke up because the basket was empty, but once I'd found her and the kittens in the bottom of your wardrobe snuggled in a jumper and put them back in the basket, she seemed quite happy to accept that's where they all had to stay.'

'In that case there *is* something else I want.' The apron was swathed around Forde's hips and the way his chest hair arrowed to his navel entranced her. He had never looked more sexy. She opened her arms, winding them round his neck when he bent down to her again and pulling him down beside her on the bed. 'I love you,' she murmured before kissing him hungrily. 'So much.'

'Words don't even begin to say what I feel for you.' He moved back slightly, taking her face between his hands as he stared into the velvet-brown of her eyes. 'You do know I'm never going to let you go again? Whatever happens in the future, whatever it holds, we walk it side by side. Mountaintop or valley, good times and bad, I'm not budging, OK?'

'OK.' She kissed him again.

'And after Christmas I'm taking you home. No argument,' he said softly.

'Me and Tabitha and her brood.' Melanie punctu-
ated each word with a kiss. 'They're ours now. I always wanted pets one day. I just didn't expect to have
four in one go.'

'We're keeping them all?'

'Of course. Tabitha deserves that.'

'And me?' Forde murmured huskily, enfolding her
against him so she could feel every inch of his hard
arousal. 'What do I deserve?'

'Everything,' she whispered throatily.

'Well, in that case...'

He kissed her until she was pulsing with desire,
bringing her to fever-pitch time and time again as he
stroked and pleasured her, caressing her until she was
trembling in his arms.

How had she managed to exist these last long, lonely
months without him? she thought wildly. But that was
all she had done: exist. This was life; being close to
Forde, feeling him, loving him. And it wasn't all about
sex, mind-blowing though that was. It was his tenderness, his care towards her, the patience and love he'd
shown ever since they'd met. Even when Matthew was
taken from them he hadn't blamed her for one moment;
putting his own feelings of grief and sorrow aside to
comfort her and be strong. She loved him so much...

She met him kiss for kiss, caress for caress, and when
he finally eased her thighs apart she was shameless in
her need of him inside her. They moved together as she
grasped him tight and close, the sheer exquisite physical pleasure taking them both to new heights. They
climaxed together in perfect unity, wave after wave of

sweet, hot gratification causing them to cry out their release.

They lay wrapped in each other's arms as they drifted back to reality, the remnants of pleasure taking some time to disperse.

Forde smiled as he traced her mouth with the tip of his finger. 'Breakfast is cold,' he murmured, kissing the tip of her small nose.

'It'll still taste good.' Anything would taste good right now. And then, as she felt the baby inside her move more vigorously than it had before, she caught his hand and placed it on her belly. 'Can you feel that?'

His face lit up. 'I think so. It's just the slightest ripple but, yes, I can feel it.'

'Our child, Forde.' And as she said it she realised the fear had gone...

CHAPTER TWELVE

IT STARTED to snow again just before lunch, but Forde
had cleared a path to the logs and coal and they were
as snug as bugs in rugs in the cottage. They spent most
of the day curled up in front of the fire watching TV
in each other's arms, eating the provisions Forde had
brought and observing Tabitha with her kittens. The
little cat was eating like a horse, seemingly intent on
making up for lost time, and all three kittens seemed
remarkably strong considering the state their mother
had been in shortly before they were born.

Mid-afternoon when the snow had stopped and the
sky had turned mother-of-pearl with streams of pure
silver, they were surprised to hear a knock at the door.
The vet stood there, her sturdy legs encased in green
wellingtons and thick trousers and her padded jacket
making her appear twice as big.

'I've just paid a visit to a farm not far from here so
I thought I'd look in,' she said cheerfully, as though
she weren't standing in half a foot of snow. 'How's the
patient?'

Melanie made her a hot drink while she examined
Tabitha and the kittens, announcing mother and babies
to be in remarkably good health considering the odds

that had been stacked against them. 'The little ginger one is a tom,' she told them, giving the kitten back to Tabitha, who began to give it a thorough clean. 'And the two black-and-white ones are females. As she seems to be getting on with being a good mother we'll leave well alone at the moment. Certainly the kittens' bellies are full and they don't appear unduly hungry or distressed.'

She downed her coffee as though she had a tin throat and left, remarking as she stepped out into the cold afternoon, 'All's well that ends well, I'm pleased to say.'

Forde held Melanie's hand very tight. 'Yes,' he said quietly. 'All's well that ends well. Merry Christmas.'

They awoke disgracefully late on Christmas Day, having gone to bed early but not to sleep. They had been both playful and intense in their lovemaking, one as eager as the other for the night not to end, until, in the early hours of the morning just before it got light, they'd gone to sleep with their arms round each other.

The morning was sparkling bright and clear, the sky icy-blue crystal and the scene outside the cottage a winter wonderland. In the far distance they could hear the faint sound of church bells ringing, and the world seemed reborn in its mantle of pure white.

Forde got up and went downstairs to check on Tabitha and make some coffee, which he brought back to bed after putting the turkey on, causing Melanie to feel deliciously lazy. Her languorous air was abruptly shattered when she saw the small but beautifully wrapped gift next to her coffee and toast, though. She shot up in bed, her voice a wail. 'Forde, I haven't got you anything. You shouldn't have.'

'Yes, I should.' He smiled at her, amused at the very feminine response. 'Besides, I had a slight advantage over you, didn't I? I knew I was coming here. I was going to leave this somewhere for you to find after I had gone,' he added softly. 'I wasn't expecting you to throw yourself on my bosom and beg for my help, nice though that was, I hasten to add.'

'What is it?'

He joined her in bed, handing the little box to her. 'See for yourself, but first—' he took her in his arms and kissed her very thoroughly '—happy Christmas, my darling.'

She undid the ribbon and pulled off the paper before lifting the lid off the box, gasping as she saw the exquisite brooch it held. The two tiny lovebirds were fashioned from precious stones forming a circle with their wings and their minute beaks were touching in a kiss. It was the most beautiful thing she had ever seen. 'Forde.' She raised shining eyes to his. 'It's so perfect. Wherever did you find it?'

'I had it specially commissioned.' He put his arm round her, kissing the tip of her nose. 'It says what I want to say every day of my life to you.'

The stones were shooting off different colours in the shaft of sunlight slanting in from the window, making the birds appear alive, and as the baby in her womb kicked suddenly Melanie had a moment of pure joy. They were going to be all right, she thought with a deep thankfulness. They had weathered the storm and come out the other side. She could believe it.

It was a perfect Christmas Day. Forde prepared the dinner while they listened to carols and Christmas songs courtesy of Melanie's CD player. He wouldn't let her lift a finger, expertly dishing up the food once it was cooked, and flaming the plum pudding with brandy and making her squeal with surprise.

Tabitha tucked into her portion of turkey and stuffing with gusto, and when Forde put down a saucerful of cream for the little cat it was clear she couldn't believe her luck. She seemed to have settled with the kittens and hadn't moved her little family again. Melanie hoped it was because Tabitha knew she was safe and secure now.

After lunch, with Tabitha and the kittens fast asleep in their basket in front of the fire in the sitting room, Melanie and Forde built a snowman in her tiny courtyard as the sun began to set in a white sky, sending rivers of red and gold and violet across the heavens. The air was bitingly cold and crisp and somewhere close a blackbird was singing its heart out, the pure notes hanging on the cold air.

For a moment Melanie knew a piercing pain that Matthew wasn't with them. He would have probably begun to toddle by now, she thought, lifting her face to the sunset. He would have loved the snow.

'You're thinking of him. I can always tell.'

She hadn't been aware that Forde was watching her, but now he enfolded her into his arms, holding her tight, as she murmured, 'I would have loved to tell him that we love him, that we'll always love him no matter how many other children we have. That he'll for ever be our precious little boy, our firstborn.'

'You'll be able to tell him that one day and give him all the cuddles and kisses you want, my love.'

'Do you believe that?' She pulled away slightly to look into his dark face. '*Really* believe it?'

'Yes, I do.' His eyes glinted down at her in the half-light. 'But for now we're here on earth and we have to get on with our lives and care for and love other children we're given. We are going to become a family when this child is born, Nell, and although the grief of losing Matthew will never fade you will learn to live with it and stop feeling guilty that you can still experience happiness and pleasure.'

'How do you know I feel like that sometimes?' she asked him, her eyes wide with surprise.

'Because I felt the same at first,' said Forde softly. 'I think all parents must in the aftermath of losing a baby or child. It's not only a terrible thing, but it's unnatural too, the wrong order in life. A parent should never outlive its child.'

She leant into him, needing his strength and understanding. 'It *will* be all right this time, won't it?' she said very quietly. 'I couldn't bear—'

'None of that.' He lifted her chin with one finger, gazing deep into her eyes. 'We are going to have a beautiful son or daughter, Nell. I promise you. Look at Tabitha and have faith, OK?'

She smiled shakily. 'People would think it was stupid to believe because one little cat made it against all the odds, it's a sign for us.'

'I don't give a damn what people think.' He pulled her more firmly into him. 'And this is Christmas, don't forget. A time for miracles and for wishes to come true. Who would have thought a few days ago we would be standing here like this, Nell? But we are. We're together again and stronger than ever before. And talking of miracles—' he touched her belly '—one night of love and this child came into being. Now, I know we would still have been together in the long run because I would never have accepted anything else, but this baby was a catalyst for you in many ways.'

His voice was so full of the relentless determination and assurance she'd come to associate with the man she loved that Melanie smiled again. 'So you're saying we're part of a Christmas miracle?'

'Dead right, we are.' He grinned, looking up into the sky. 'Look at that. It's specially for us, you know. A true modern-art spectacular.'

Melanie giggled. 'You're crazy—you know that, don't you?'

'For you? Guilty as charged.' He turned her to look at their snowman, who was definitely something of a cross-dresser, having one of Melanie's scarves tied round his neck—a pink, fluffy number with tiny sequins sewn into it—and one of her summer straw hats complete with ribbons and tiny daisies. 'Is he finished?'

'Just about.'

'Then I suggest we go inside and warm up.'

'In front of the fire with a mug of hot chocolate?'

'Possibly.' He eyed her sexily. 'Not quite what I had in mind, though. I was thinking of something more… cosy.'

'More cosy than hot chocolate?' she murmured, pretending ignorance.

'As in one hundred per cent.'

'Oh, well, in that case…'

'And remember.' He took her cold face in his hands,

suddenly serious. 'I love you and you love me. Anything else—*anything*—comes second to that.'

Melanie nodded. She wanted to believe that. She *needed* to. And perhaps that was what this was all about: a step of faith. She linked her arms round his neck. 'I love Christmas.'

He kissed her forehead, dislodging her bright scarlet pom-pom hat in the process. 'Best time of the year,' he said huskily. 'The very best.'

CHAPTER THIRTEEN

MELANIE was remembering the magic of Christmas as Forde drove her to the hospital in the last week of May.

The weather couldn't have been more different. For weeks the country had been enjoying warm, sunny days more typical of the Mediterranean, and James and the assistant she had hired to help him had been rushed off their feet with work. Business was booming and already her small company had a reputation for excellent reliability and first-class results, which boded well for the future. But Melanie wasn't thinking of James or the company as Forde's Aston Martin ate up the miles to the hospital; she was lost in the enchantment of those days when she and Forde had been enclosed in their own isolated world, along with Tabitha and the kittens, of course.

The kittens had grown swiftly into little cats developing distinct personalities of their own. They had named the two little females Holly and Ivy, and the larger boy Noel, and it was a good thing Tabitha was something of a strict mother because the three could be quite a handful. But Melanie loved them passionately and because love begot love, they loved her back, even if it was in the somewhat superior feline version of that emotion.

Her favourite was Tabitha though. The little tabby was devoted to Melanie in the same way a dog would be, following her about the house and liking nothing more than to lie at her feet or on her lap whenever she could. She kept her troublesome threesome under control by a swift tap of the paw now and again and the odd warning growl when they stepped out of line, but on the whole it was a happy household.

It was Tabitha who was at the forefront of Melanie's mind as she said, 'You made sure the cats were all in before we left?'

'Absolutely.' Forde's voice was indulgent. She had asked him the same question twice before. 'And the TV's off and the back door's locked. OK?'

Melanie smiled at him. She had been in labour for some hours but the contractions had followed no particular pattern and there had been no urgency about them. Then, with a suddenness that had surprised her and panicked Forde, they'd increased dramatically in intensity with considerably less time between them.

Her overnight bag had been packed for weeks and left in the same place, at the foot of their bed, but somehow Forde had been unable to find it until she had lent a hand. She glanced now at the speedometer, her voice deliberately casual when she said, 'We're doing fifty in a thirty zone, Forde.'

'I know.' His voice was a little strained.

'There's plenty of time.' But even as she spoke a new contraction gripped her, her muscles tightening until it was nigh on unbearable before loosening again.

'OK?' Forde hadn't slowed one iota and the glance

he shot at her was desperate. 'I told you we should have left hours ago, Nell.'

'It's fine.' She was able to smile again. 'Three of the mothers from the antenatal classes were sent home again due to false alarms and I'd just die if that was me. I wanted to make sure.'

Forde groaned. 'Would having the baby in the car convince you?' And then realising that wasn't the most tactful of remarks, he added quickly, 'Not that we wouldn't cope with that, of course, if it happened, but I'd prefer you to be in hospital.'

She would too, actually. And she was beginning to think she might have left it a little late—not that she'd admit that to Forde. Not the way he was driving.

Melanie focused her thoughts on the baby, willing herself to be calm and composed. They had decided they didn't want to know the sex of their child at the twenty-week scan at the beginning of the year. It didn't matter. The only thing that was important was that the baby was healthy after all.

They arrived at the hospital in a violet twilight that was balmy and scented with summer, but for once Melanie was oblivious to the beauty of the flowering bushes surrounding the car park as another contraction held her stomach in a vice. She held onto Forde at the side of the car as it gathered steam and then began to pant like an animal, her nails digging into his flesh.

'I'll go and get a wheelchair,' he said, glancing round with a hunted expression on his face as though one were going to pop into his vision any moment. 'Sit back in the car.'

She held onto him with all her strength until the contraction was over and then said firmly, 'I am most certainly not using a wheelchair, Forde Masterson. They're four minutes apart so we can get to Reception before the next one and then I can wait a while before we go to the maternity unit.'

He looked at her with huge admiration. Since she had returned home with him after they had spent Christmas in the cottage, she had taken everything in her stride. He had to admit he had been like a cat on a hot tin roof the past couple of weeks waiting for the baby to come, but Melanie had been what he could only call serene. They had decorated the nursery in pale lemon and cream eight weeks ago and everything was ready for the new arrival. They just needed the baby now. His stomach jumped with excitement mixed with concern for Melanie. He hadn't expected her to be in such pain, although perhaps he should have.

They didn't make Reception before the next contraction had her clinging onto him. Now fear was added to the mix. He had visions of the baby being born in the car park and delivering it himself. He should have made her come to the hospital earlier, he told himself desperately as Melanie's fingers fastened on his wrists like steel bands. But she was so damn stubborn. And wonderful and beautiful and amazing.

After what seemed an eternity her grip lessened, although he could see beads of perspiration on her brow. 'Wow.' She smiled shakily. 'Do you remember what they told us in the classes if the baby comes unexpectedly?'

'Don't,' he said weakly.

He half carried her the rest of the way and once they stepped through the massive glass doors into Reception the hospital machine took over with an efficiency Forde was thankful for. In no time they'd been whisked along to the maternity unit and placed in a delivery room. For a moment he remembered the last time they had been in the unit and his guts twisted, but when he looked at Melanie she was concentrating on following the midwife's instructions. He stared at her face, at her total look of concentration and the courage she was displaying, and his world swung back onto its axis.

'You're doing fine, sweetheart,' he murmured, wishing he could share the pain. 'Not long now.'

In fact the contractions continued at three-minute intervals for the next two hours, which seemed a lifetime to Forde, although the hospital staff didn't seem unduly concerned.

Melanie was getting tired, even dozing between one contraction and the next in the couple of minutes' respite, but she still held onto his hand with the strength of a dozen women and every so often would smile and tell him everything was all right. He felt helpless, badgering the midwife once or twice until that good lady sent him a look like a dagger.

Then, suddenly, a little while after midnight, everything speeded up. Melanie began pushing and another midwife joined them, the two women stationed either side of Melanie's bent legs while he sat by the bed holding her hand. He wouldn't have thought she had enough strength left for what was required but as ever she proved him wrong, pushing with all her might when the midwives told her to push and panting like an animal again when they told her to stop.

Twenty minutes later their son was born and he was

a whopper, according to the midwife who immediately placed him in Melanie's arms. Forde knew if he lived to be a hundred he would never forget the expression on Melanie's face as she gazed into the little screwed-up face. And the baby looked back with bright blue-grey eyes as if he knew his mother already. 'Hello, you,' she whispered softly, the tears running down her face as she kissed his velvety brow. 'I'm your mummy, my precious darling. And this is your daddy.' She turned to Forde with a radiant smile to see his cheeks were wet too.

'He's so beautiful.' Forde kissed her tenderly before offering his finger to his son, who immediately grasped it with surprising strength, making them both laugh. 'And look at all that black hair.'

'He's going to be as handsome as his father,' said one of the midwives, beaming at them both and their transparent wonder at the little person they had created. 'My, he's a bonny lad and no mistake. Over ten pounds, I'll be bound.'

In actual fact, Luke Forde Masterson weighed in at ten pounds nine ounces—something, Melanie said in an aside and with great feeling, that didn't surprise her.

The midwives bustled off, promising to return in a few minutes with a cup of tea for them both. Melanie sat cradling her son with Forde perched on the bed at her side, his arm round her shoulders.

'How do you feel?' he said very softly as she stroked one tiny cheek with the tip of her finger.

She didn't try to prevaricate. 'Wonderful,' she said equally softly, 'and a tiny bit sad, but that's only natural, I suppose. It doesn't mean I love Luke any the less, just that I wish things had been different with Matthew.'

He nodded, his arm tightening for a moment.

'Isn't he beautiful, Forde? And he already looks like you,' she went on. 'He's got your nose. Can you see it?'

Forde looked at his son. He *was* beautiful, certainly the most beautiful child in the whole of England, but he simply looked like a baby, he thought, wondering how women could say these things and genuinely see what most men couldn't. He smiled. 'I'd prefer him to look like you.'

'Oh, no.' She shook her head. 'Our daughters will look like me and our sons like you.'

After what she had just been through he found it amazing she could talk of having more children just at that moment. He kissed her hard on the lips. 'I love you, Mrs Masterson.'

'And I love you, Mr Masterson. Always.'

EPILOGUE

MELANIE and Forde went on to have the family they had dreamed of. Eighteen months after Luke was born, twin girls—Amy Melanie and Sophie Isabelle—made their appearance. True to Melanie's prediction the girls were the very image of their lovely mother. And two years after that another boy, John William—William had been Forde's father's name—made their family complete.

They had left the house in Kingston upon Thames just after the twins were born, moving to a huge old Elizabethan mansion in the country, which had acres of land attached to it along with magnificent gardens that would delight any child. It even came with a fine tree house built in one of the giant oak trees a little distance from the house, and this was nearly as big as Melanie's little cottage. She hadn't been able to bear to sell the cottage, not with all the memories it held of the wonderful Christmas when she and Forde had come together again, and now James had taken up residence there. With Melanie's growing family he had taken a larger part in the running of the firm, which had continued to go from strength to strength. James had three full-time employees and two part-time under his direction, along with a middle-aged lady who had taken on most of the paperwork involved with the company.

Tabitha and her little family had been joined by two rescue dogs—the cats ruling the roost with iron paws— and as time went on the children had a couple of small ponies so they could learn to ride, and an aged donkey— again a rescue animal—that Melanie wanted to end its days in comfort with others of its kind for company.

It was a happy household, but when John started school Melanie felt it was time to put an idea to Forde that had been in the back of her mind for a long time. Isabelle had been living with them for the past few years, having become too frail to continue in her own home, but sadly had died in the spring, peacefully though and in her own bed.

Melanie and Forde were sitting by the swimming pool Forde had had built shortly after they had moved to the house. They were watching the children and some of the children's friends playing in the water before Forde organised a barbecue for lunch. It was a beautiful summer's day at the beginning of June, the sky high and cornflower-blue without a cloud to be seen, and the scents from the garden intoxicating.

Melanie took a deep breath and turned to Forde, who was lying on the sunlounger next to hers clad only in his swimming shorts. As always when she looked at him, her pulse quickened. His body was as taut and lean as it had ever been and he oozed sex appeal, which was all the more potent for his unawareness of his devastating attractiveness. She deposited a long kiss on his sexy, uneven mouth before settling back on her own lounger. 'I need to talk to you.'

He smiled, his silver-blue eyes crinkling. 'You don't need to make an appointment, sweetheart. We are married, remember?'

Oh, yes, she remembered all right. The heavenly nights of bliss in their huge bed were a constant reminder.

'This is serious, Forde. I want us to start long-term fostering, taking in the sort of troubled child I was, the sort no one else is really keen to have.'

Forde sat up straighter.

'Now John's started school and your mother's gone, I feel it's the right time. When I was nursing Isabelle I felt she needed all my attention and a peaceful life at her age, but now that's not a consideration any more.'

Forde looked at his wife. He never tired of looking at her. He thought she got younger with every passing year, the joy of family life turning her into a female Peter Pan. 'Are you sure about this?' he asked quietly. 'It would mean huge changes and it won't be easy some of the time. The children would have to make some adjustments too.'

Melanie nodded. He hadn't said no outright. 'I know that. This isn't a whim, believe me. As for our children, you know I love them beyond words and they will always come first. But...' She paused, finding the right words. 'They have no idea of the unhappiness some children live with every day of their lives, and I'm glad they don't know that for themselves, of course I am, but sharing their home—and us—with such children will make our four better human beings in the long run. They are privileged, Forde, so privileged, and I'm grateful for that, but I don't want them to grow up without understanding everyone's not as fortunate as they are.

I—I remember how it was for me as a child and I want to give something back. I want to help such little ones, give them a chance to feel wanted and loved. This is such a big house with wonderful grounds and we have four spare guest rooms we rarely use.'

Forde frowned. 'What about the sheer mechanics of caring for more children, giving them adequate time and attention? I can be around more but not all the time and I don't want you worked into the ground, Nell. It was hard work with my mother towards the end when she got very poorly and, although this will be different, you'll need help.'

'I know that.' She was trying very hard to keep the excitement out of her voice but nevertheless it sneaked in. 'And part of what makes me feel this is the time to do it is that I spoke to Janet the other day. You know we meet for lunch a couple of times a year?'

Forde nodded. It had been too far for Janet to travel when they had moved house, besides which Melanie had been keen to take over the role of full-time mother and housewife, which was why she had given most of the running of the business into James's capable hands. But she hadn't lost contact with their old housekeeper, meeting her occasionally and sending huge hampers to the house every Christmas.

'Well, her husband died last year as you know, and two of her children are married now and have left home. The girl that's left is the one with learning difficulties but she's great at cooking and cleaning like her mother. It's a rented house and I know Janet would love to come here as housekeeper and cook with her daughter helping her. Between the three of us we could run the house fine, and having Janet and her daughter here would free me up to take care of our children and any we foster, with Janet available as a back-up in any emergency. It would work, Forde. I know it would. But you have to want it too, I know that.'

'Where would Janet and her daughter live? In the granny annexe we built for Mother?'

'Would you mind that?'

'Of course not.' He ran a hand through his hair as he did when he was anxious or thoughtful. 'But I'd have to look into this more fully. *We* would have to look into it more fully.'

'Absolutely.'

'There'll be checks and red tape and who knows what. It'll mean opening up every area of our life to strangers before we could get a go-ahead.'

'I know that too but it would be worth it. I'd like to try, Forde. If nothing else I'd like us to try. If it doesn't happen—' she shrugged '—so be it.'

A slow smile spread over his rugged features. 'Nell, I know you well enough by now to know you don't mean a word of that. This is important to you, isn't it?'

'It is but unless you're completely happy we won't go ahead about even finding out the ins and outs.'

He leaned towards her, touching her cheek with his hand. 'If it's important to you it's important to me— you know that.'

When he looked at her like that all she wanted to do was fling herself into his arms and ravish him. She contented herself with cupping his face in her palms and kissing him deeply and passionately. 'So I can go ahead and make some enquiries?'

Lifting her left hand to his lips, Forde pressed a gentle kiss on the finger that held her wedding and engagement rings. 'We'll do it together at every stage, OK?'

'OK,' Melanie whispered, wanting him, loving him.

Social Services welcomed them with open arms. As Forde had forecast the red tape stretched for ever, however, but by Christmas they had all the necessary pieces of paper in place and their initial two children, a boy and a girl who weren't related but had spent some time together in short-term care, had arrived to spend the Christmas holiday with them to see how they all got on.

The children's case histories were dire and there was no doubt they regarded all adults with deep distrust and, in the boy's case, a great deal of pent-up anger, but from the moment Melanie saw their small, wary faces she loved them. They came to the house a couple of days before Christmas and on Christmas Eve Melanie sat on the boy's bed and told him a story of a little girl who had been in care and who felt abandoned and alone. He listened with hostile eyes until the moment she told him she had been that little girl, and then it was clear she had taken him aback.

It was the breakthrough she had prayed for. From being surly and suspicious he began to ask her question after question and in so doing some of his own traumatic history came out quite naturally. The rest of the children were fast asleep, waiting for Santa to fill their stockings, and Melanie spent two hours talking to him before he settled down to sleep.

When she joined Forde downstairs, he reached out a hand to her, drawing her towards the French windows and opening them so the crisp, biting air caressed their faces. A few desultory snowflakes were beginning to fall on the sparkling ground, which was white with frost, and the trees surrounding the house looked breathtakingly beautiful in their mantle of white. 'A fresh new world,' he murmured softly, drawing her tight into his side. 'And that's what I want for these children, Nell. I crept up and listened at the bedroom door while you were talking to him and I know you're going to transform his life.'

'We both are,' she said softly, emotion making her voice husky.

'But you most of all.' He smiled, kissing her hard. 'We're going to have more Christmas miracles, Nell, and our family is going to grow in a way I hadn't thought of but which is perfect. Because of you, my love. All because of you. What did I ever do to deserve you?'

'That's what I think every time I look at you,' she whispered. 'You didn't let me go when I walked away. You came after me. You will never know what that meant.'

'We won't let these little ones go either.' He looked up into the pearly gray sky from which more and more snowflakes were falling. 'This is going to be another wonderful Christmas, my darling.'

And it was.

* * * * *

Mills & Boon® Hardback

September 2012

ROMANCE

Unlocking her Innocence	Lynne Graham
Santiago's Command	Kim Lawrence
His Reputation Precedes Him	Carole Mortimer
The Price of Retribution	Sara Craven
Just One Last Night	Helen Brooks
The Greek's Acquisition	Chantelle Shaw
The Husband She Never Knew	Kate Hewitt
When Only Diamonds Will Do	Lindsay Armstrong
The Couple Behind the Headlines	Lucy King
The Best Mistake of Her Life	Aimee Carson
The Valtieri Baby	Caroline Anderson
Slow Dance with the Sheriff	Nikki Logan
Bella's Impossible Boss	Michelle Douglas
The Tycoon's Secret Daughter	Susan Meier
She's So Over Him	Joss Wood
Return of the Last McKenna	Shirley Jump
Once a Playboy...	Kate Hardy
Challenging the Nurse's Rules	Janice Lynn

MEDICAL

Her Motherhood Wish	Anne Fraser
A Bond Between Strangers	Scarlet Wilson
The Sheikh and the Surrogate Mum	Meredith Webber
Tamed by her Brooding Boss	Joanna Neil

Mills & Boon® Large Print

September 2012

ROMANCE

A Vow of Obligation	Lynne Graham
Defying Drakon	Carole Mortimer
Playing the Greek's Game	Sharon Kendrick
One Night in Paradise	Maisey Yates
Valtieri's Bride	Caroline Anderson
The Nanny Who Kissed Her Boss	Barbara McMahon
Falling for Mr Mysterious	Barbara Hannay
The Last Woman He'd Ever Date	Liz Fielding
His Majesty's Mistake	Jane Porter
Duty and the Beast	Trish Morey
The Darkest of Secrets	Kate Hewitt

HISTORICAL

Lady Priscilla's Shameful Secret	Christine Merrill
Rake with a Frozen Heart	Marguerite Kaye
Miss Cameron's Fall from Grace	Helen Dickson
Society's Most Scandalous Rake	Isabelle Goddard
The Taming of the Rogue	Amanda McCabe

MEDICAL

Falling for the Sheikh She Shouldn't	Fiona McArthur
Dr Cinderella's Midnight Fling	Kate Hardy
Brought Together by Baby	Margaret McDonagh
One Month to Become a Mum	Louisa George
Sydney Harbour Hospital: Luca's Bad Girl	Amy Andrews
The Firebrand Who Unlocked His Heart	Anne Fraser

Mills & Boon® Hardback

October 2012

ROMANCE

MEDICAL

ROMANCE

A Secret Disgrace	Penny Jordan
The Dark Side of Desire	Julia James
The Forbidden Ferrara	Sarah Morgan
The Truth Behind his Touch	Cathy Williams
Plain Jane in the Spotlight	Lucy Gordon
Battle for the Soldier's Heart	Cara Colter
The Navy SEAL's Bride	Soraya Lane
My Greek Island Fling	Nina Harrington
Enemies at the Altar	Melanie Milburne
In the Italian's Sights	Helen Brooks
In Defiance of Duty	Caitlin Crews

HISTORICAL

The Duchess Hunt	Elizabeth Beacon
Marriage of Mercy	Carla Kelly
Unbuttoning Miss Hardwick	Deb Marlowe
Chained to the Barbarian	Carol Townend
My Fair Concubine	Jeannie Lin

MEDICAL

Georgie's Big Greek Wedding?	Emily Forbes
The Nurse's Not-So-Secret Scandal	Wendy S. Marcus
Dr Right All Along	Joanna Neil
Summer With A French Surgeon	Margaret Barker
Sydney Harbour Hospital: Tom's Redemption	Fiona Lowe
Doctor on Her Doorstep	Annie Claydon